SHADOW OVER FLODDEN

SHADOW OVER FLODDEN

Mary Cummins

Chivers Press • G.K. Hall & Co.
Bath, England   Thorndike, Maine USA

This Large Print edition is published by Chivers Press, England, and by G.K. Hall & Co., USA.

Published in 1998 in the U.K. by arrangement with Robert Hale Ltd.

Published in 1997 in the U.S. by arrangement with Robert Hale Ltd.

U.K. Hardcover ISBN 0–7540–3028–8 (Chivers Large Print)
U.S. Softcover ISBN 0–7838–8217–3 (Nightingale Collection Edition)

Copyright © Mary Cummins 1985

All rights reserved.

The text of this Large Print edition is unabridged.
Other aspects of the book may vary from the original edition.

Set in 16 pt. New Times Roman.

Printed in Great Britain on acid-free paper.

British Library Cataloguing in Publication Data available

Library of Congress Cataloging-in-Publication Data

Cummins, Mary.
  Shadow over Flodden / Mary Cummins.
    p. cm.
  ISBN 0–7838–8217–3 (lg. print : sc : alk. paper)
  1. Large type books. I. Title
[PR6073.A72265S53   1997]
823'.914—dc21   97–18508

CHAPTER ONE

Now that it was early September, the weather had grown cooler and a snell wind was blowing in from the east.

Mistress Sarah Graham had ordered that a fire be lit in the Great Hall so that her grandmother could enjoy its warmth. It now belched smoke along the stone corridors but Lady Margaret only huddled the closer. Her bony limbs were growing riddled with rheumatism and she needed the warmth to ease the joints. Not even the potions which Anna Hyslop brewed in the kitchens seemed to ease the pain and she grew more querulous every day.

'I can hear the boy,' she complained to Sarah. 'John Dykes allows him to do as he will. He spoils the lad.'

'He has only brought Jamie indoors for a bite of meat, Grandmother,' said Sarah, patiently. 'It is an hour before we have supper and growing boys need nourishment. Jamie is only six.'

'His father was near a man at six,' said Lady Margaret, then her face crinkled into a smile. She truly loved her only grandson who was heir to Larraig, a good rich barony, if small. The land was fertile and its position on the banks of the Forth, west of Stirling, was as fair as any in Scotland.

Lady Margaret sighed and looked into the rising smoke, thinking that she might not see another winter. She was old, old and tired. It was the women who had to keep the castle these days, but they had learned to do so with competence and dignity, just as she had ensured that her granddaughter, Sarah, knew how to conduct herself.

It was time Thomas was back home. He had ridden out with a band of their best men to follow the King south in order to do battle with the English under King Henry, the Queen's brother. It was not a popular battle, thought Lady Margaret, shaking her head. Along with many others, Thomas had advised King James against a quarrel with the English king, and a night or two before riding out, he had come to see her as she lay in the huge four-poster bed in which she rested most of her days.

It had then been August, 1513, but there had been a spell of wet weather and Lady Margaret had become more disabled as a result of the damp humid atmosphere in the old castle.

'You need to rebuild, Thomas,' she had told him. 'We are not now quarrelling with the Drummonds so we need not fortify Larraig as though it were a Border Keep. Many places have good walls and glass windows these days, as well as carpets and fine cabinets. They say the cabinet-makers in Edinburgh are as good as any in Europe, and we need somewhere to display the glass your father brought back from Venice.'

'Little use it is,' Sir Thomas grumbled. 'The maidservants fear to dust it in case it breaks. My lady, Helen, was not concerned with such things.'

'Aye ... maybe.'

Lady Margaret's tone dropped. Her daughter-in-law had been a handsome enough woman and a good wife for Thomas, but she had spent more time at her loom than seeing to it that Larraig was well served. She had borne a fine daughter, Sarah, seventeen years ago, then she had lost three sons. But when Jamie was born, she had also lost her own life and Lady Margaret had taken over the running of Larraig once more.

Sarah had been sent to Edinburgh to serve Queen Margaret, and to help tend the little Prince Jamie who was now seventeen months old. Sarah had been well used to helping with her own brother, Jamie, and she was good with the child. Queen Margaret had quickly seen that the girl could keep the child entertained, and had appointed her as an assistant nursemaid to Jane Hamilton.

Lady Margaret Graham had managed Larraig for her son, having already set the servants a high standard over the years. Her husband, James, had been killed in battle at Sauchieburn and she had warned Thomas to remember this when he rode out to join the

King. Latest rumours said that James commanded a strong army, having mustered his men at Twizel Bridge near Kelso.

'It is all very well to give the English a dunt, Thomas,' she said, 'but only a righteous anger against them for something we cannot thole justifies the shedding of blood. I hope you know what you are fighting for.'

She had been having bad dreams which left her feeling that their household was threatened, and especially her granddaughter, Sarah, but Thomas would not listen to such tales. He stretched out his long, hose-clad legs as he sat by his mother's bedside. He wore a heavy linen shirt over a velvet jerkin, and far below, in the courtyard, the sounds of activity came to them clearly as horses were saddled, provisions packed and preparations made for a long journey.

'I do not mind giving King Henry a dunt,' he said. 'He is not like his father, our good Queen's father, that is. Now *he* promised us a fine dowry for her, but the son does not know how to honour the word of the father. We have to depend on the goodness of our French ally when our coffers run short, and now King Henry has marched into France and our King has to give Louis a bit of help, Mother.'

'Aye.' Her voice was suddenly dry. 'I have heard tell that the new Queen of France ... she who was Anne, Duchess of Brittany is even bonnier than Louis's first Queen, Jeanne. She has sent our King a ring and has asked him to march three miles into England for her sake. Some said she was calling herself his lady-love, no less. I wonder what Queen Margaret thinks of that!'

'It is only chivalry on his part, though maybe he is a bit quick to take it up.'

'It is not worth your life, Thomas.'

'I must serve my King, Lady, like my father before me. I am pledged to do that.'

She sighed deeply. 'I see your father in you, but you are a better fighter than he ever was. Do not worry about young Jamie. Sarah is coming home to help me with him, since my old bones are likely to crack any day, but keep in mind that tale about the man in the azure-blue gown who visited the King at his prayers. Aye, azure-blue they said it was, with a linen girdle. He had long yellow hair and sandals on his feet and he said his mother had sent him. He told the King not to make the journey, then he vanished clean away, Thomas. I had the story from Neil Drummond of Balwhidden, Thomas, who saw it with his own eyes. He was at Linlithgow with the King and they were at their devotions at the time. Now, who was that man, Thomas? That's what I would like to know.'

'Maybe it is a rumour. There are plenty of them.'

'Do you doubt Balwhidden? He cannot do battle because he only has one arm, but his sons will not listen to him either.'

Thomas shook his head and moved uneasily. No, he did not doubt Drummond of Balwhidden, their own neighbour, but if the King was not going to pay attention to such a man bringing him a warning, why should he? But ... a long azure-blue gown, girt with linen ... long yellow hair ... now that certainly was not an ordinary figure!

'I should have arranged a marriage for Sarah before I go,' he said.

His eyes were on his mother's slender white hand, now deformed with arthritis, and a coldness lay on his heart. His daughter was young and beautiful, but after he rode out there would be no man to hold Larraig in trust for Jamie. He should have talked with Drummond and made a match for her with one of his two sons ... Archibald, maybe, since he was the heir. It would be no bad thing for Larraig and Balwhidden to be administered jointly. They had been friends for two generations now and no bitterness in their hearts for past quarrels. Land had been agreed and Sir Neil Drummond was happy as he was himself, though Balwhidden was the greater barony.

But Larraig was older and their history went deep. Sarah would make a fine bride for a Drummond.

'What are you thinking now?' his mother asked, her eyes gleaming like coal-black beads.

'Sarah. I should have married her to Archibald Drummond.'

She smiled briefly. 'Sarah has a mind of her own and I have seen a look in her eyes when she talks about young Douglas, grandson to Angus, who hangs around the Court and is very courtly to the Queen when the King is away. I am concerned about that, Thomas.'

'Douglas! But he is one of the highest in the land! She is my daughter and I think her a match for any man, but can you see old "Bell-the-Cat" consenting to a marriage between his grandson and a lass like Sarah? No, no, she will have to put him out of her mind.'

'That she will,' said Lady Margaret, and heaved a great sigh. Sometimes when love touched the heart of a woman, it was not easy to put the man out of your mind!

Sarah had ridden home with two strong men as escorts before her father left to join the King at Twizel Bridge and Thomas had been surprised and his heart touched to see that his daughter had grown into such a fine young lady under the influence of Queen Margaret's court.

The country was a poor one compared with England and France, but the people were well-fed with good meat, plenty of fish and oats, and wild fruits. In France he had nearly given a fellow a thick ear for calling his beloved country 'Fishy Scotland', but there was no doubt that they had fish a-plenty.

The King had encouraged foreigners to settle down in the country and people were being taught new trades and manufactures so that the ladies lived more graciously than they had done even when Lady Margaret was a girl. The money borrowed from France had been put to good use.

But perhaps all this fine living had not fitted Sarah to fend for herself, thought Thomas worriedly as he took leave of her, and his strong little son, Jamie.

'Look to them as long as you can, Lady,' he said to his mother as he clasped her thin fingers in his own strong hands.

'Away, then, if you must go!' she told him, gruffly.

As usual, she had been spending an extra hour or two in bed, but she crawled out and watched from the narrow window and could not hold the difficult tears as she saw him ride out with his men. Often her husband and son had both gone with scoldings and prayers on her lips, but this time there was only a numb ache, which coursed the tears down her cheeks. This time they had little cause to fight for, except love of their King.

She heard the chatter of young Jamie as he climbed the stairs with Sarah close behind him, followed by the clatter of their feet on the stone corridor. They needed a better house with solid floors on polished wood and good glass windows in the bedrooms, such as Drummond had built at Balwhidden, then her knees would not feel the cold so readily, thought Lady Margaret crossly, hoping that her anger could blot out the sorrow in her heart. She did not want Sarah to see that her courage was deserting her.

'So they have gone,' she said to Sarah.

'Mungo Foreman promised to let me hold his pike,' Jamie was protesting, tears beginning to glisten, 'then my sister took me away. She says there was no time.'

'Be quiet, Jamie!' Sarah said, sternly.

She and her grandmother avoided one another's eyes. They both had bad feelings about these latest troubles.

'Can I leave Jamie with you, Grandmother?' she asked. 'I have to see to the suppers for—for we who are left.'

'Come up here and sit on my bed, boy, and I will tell you a story,' Lady Margaret commanded.

Her black eyes showed respect for the tall young woman who had seemed to grow overnight from girlhood to womanhood. She had shed the soft silks and velvets which she wore at court when she was away from her duties, and now wore a home-spun woollen gown with a linen overdress. She had shed her fashionable tall headdress, worn over two horns, and bound up her fair hair under a cap. Sarah had inherited that golden hair from her mother, Helen, but her black eyes were exactly like those of her grandmother, and sometimes blazed with the same humours. Perhaps Thomas need not have such fears for her, thought Lady Margaret, as she turned to the child.

'Once upon a time there was a great King of Scotland called Robert the Bruce...'

'And the spider,' said the child.

'Aye, but that comes afterwards. Settle down and let me tell it in my own way.'

CHAPTER TWO

Why did everything have to change so quickly? Sarah wondered as she checked their stores with John Dykes. She had thought to remain at Court until she was obliged to please her father by marrying a man of his choice, or ... or ...

Sarah Graham's face glowed rosily in a burnished mirror. Douglas had often stayed at Court in the absence of the King, ostensibly to assist Queen Margaret if some personal matter required to be resolved. He was tall and very handsome, and he attended diligently to the Queen's every wish.

He had taken a great interest in young Prince James and made his way often to the nursery quarters, ignoring the authority of Lady Jane

Hamilton who was in charge of the young Prince.

'He is newly bedded this minute, my Lord Douglas,' Lady Jane told him. 'You will not disturb his rest.'

'I have promised the Queen that I shall admire the Prince,' Lord Douglas said, carelessly, then smiled. Few people could resist his smile, but Lady Jane was a Hamilton and they were not over fond of the Douglases.

His grandfather, Archibald Douglas, Earl of Angus, had also been a handsome man and it was known that he favoured this grandson who was brave and courageous, even as he was handsome.

But he was also rash and inclined to be imprudent, thought Lady Jane, shrewdly. She did not like the way he looked at the Queen, but her Majesty would have raised one of her arched eyebrows if anyone had dropped a warning in her ear. She only lived for news of the King, but she deplored his absence on this occasion. She had implored James not to go out challenging his brother-in-law to war.

'Why not?' James had demanded. 'Where is his honour? He has never paid your dowry, being one of many insults, and knowing that I allowed for the money when planning improvements in running the country. Now that he has taken his army to France, I sent my herald with a letter to him at Terouenne, asking him to reconsider any battle with

France. You have heard his answer, Madam, that I, the King of Scotland, am not of sufficient importance to determine the quarrel between England and France. What do you say to that? Besides...'

'Besides you are full of chivalry, James, and that is admired by the Queen of France. I have heard that she is young and beautiful.'

James's ready temper began to rise.

'It is no insult to be recognized for chivalry,' he told her. 'But I cannot take your brother's insults any longer.'

Now it was young Douglas to whom the Queen must turn, and when he strode into the nursery and lifted the baby Prince James into his arms, Sarah Graham turned from folding away the child's clean linen and her heart bounded like a trapped bird. Never had she seen a more handsome man, nor one so bold. She had seen him attending the Queen, but had tended to keep her eyes down, shyly, in his presence so that he rarely spoke to her directly. Now he stood beside her, a powerful figure, strong and stalwart.

'I ride out to join the King,' he said. 'I must take news of the Queen and his son. He will want to know if the child cuts his teeth, or if he can yet speak a word.'

'A word or two,' said Sarah, 'and three more teeth in the past two weeks.'

'Truly a remarkable child,' Douglas told her, 'but then he has a remarkable father, and mother.'

'Aye, sir,' said Sarah, blushing.

The young nobleman's eyes had swept over her boldly.

'I shall come and see him again when I return,' he said, though his eyes promised that it might be Sarah, herself, who could be the main attraction.

He put the child on to his cot where he immediately bounced on to his knees and began to cry peevishly and rub his nose with the back of his small fat hand.

'Over-tired now, that's what he is,' Lady Jane grumbled. 'He has been wakened out of his sleep.'

'Then put him back to sleep,' Douglas told her, impatiently. Again he nodded to Sarah.

'Take care of the boy. He...' he hesitated and pulled a lock of hair thoughtfully, '... he is a precious child. He will no doubt be King... one day...'

'More than *you* will ever be,' Lady Jane had muttered, darkly, when she was sure Douglas was well away from the chamber. 'No one can ever convince the Douglases that they are not royalty, and have them believe it, yet they are no better than the Hamiltons. My kinsman, the Earl of Arran, is as high as any Douglas.'

'My father says that if our nobles stopped fighting with one another and being jealous of one another, we would all be better off,' said Sarah. She did not want to hear the noble young lord criticized.

'Well, they have more to fight with now than each other,' Jane Hamilton told her, roundly, 'and that includes your father, Sir Thomas Graham. I hear that you are recalled to Larraig, Mistress Sarah.'

'Recalled?' Sarah stared at her.

'The Queen informed me. Sir Thomas requests that you be allowed to go home. He rides out for the King and your grandmother is too sick to hold Larraig. You have your own child to mind, your brother James.'

Sarah busied herself with the linen. A few months ago she would have been delighted to be going home, but now ... but now ... She bit her lip as she acknowledged the truth to herself. She might never see Lord Douglas again, and that would leave a sad ache in her heart.

Yet he was not for her, she reminded herself. Nothing less than a princess would be good enough for the grandson of Bell-the-Cat, Archibald Douglas. She was stupid to allow her heart to be touched by the briefest contact with that nobleman, but how could she help it? Even the Queen often remarked that he was a very handsome fellow.

'When must I go?' she asked Lady Jane.

'The sooner the better, child, though I shall miss you. Isabel Grant is a flighty young woman and too fond of herself to soil her hands. She has no patience with my wee mannie, whilst you love him as though he were your brother.'

'That is true,' said Sarah. 'He is a lovely child.'

'Your father is sending a couple of strong men as escort though you have not got too far to go. The King wants the court to move to Stirling before winter. We catch the snell winds in Edinburgh, even if it is now declared the capital city of our realm. You could travel to Stirling and the escort will meet you there. Tell your grandmother that I send my felicitations. I knew Margaret Graham well in our young days. We were in many a prank together.' Jane Hamilton smiled reminiscently. 'She was a handsome woman.'

Sighing she lifted a box of herbal waters and ointments designed to keep coughs and colds at bay for the young Prince.

'No more day-dreaming and keep that young nobleman out of your thoughts. Oh, he is a fine gentleman, I grant you that, but there is something about him I do not trust. He is too fond of himself.'

Sarah made no reply. She doubted if any Douglas would please a Hamilton.

* * *

Now she was home again, and how small and shabby Larraig seemed after the more gracious rooms at Court. Some people frowned on the fact that James IV spent freely of the money his father had saved, in addition to what he borrowed, on providing gracious living for himself and his family, but there was no doubt that it contributed greatly to one's comfort, thought Sarah, as she walked through the rooms at Larraig which were clean enough, but hardly luxurious. Even her grandmother advocated that something could be done.

'Our farmers live more comfortably than we do,' she often remarked to Sir Thomas, and he promised to attend to the matter as soon as the King had settled his quarrel with his brother-in-law, King Henry.

How long would that take? wondered Sarah, as she bade the maidservants seek out a ham which had not been sufficiently well smoked. The smell was unmistakable, and Sarah hoped that a quantity of it would not be affected. Going over the stores now with John Dykes, she saw that they were becoming short of provisions.

'Sir Thomas and most of our best men have been on the saddle,' John Dykes reminded her, 'and Lady Margaret huddles close to the fire. We have to do our best, Mistress.'

'I will attend to it,' Sarah told him. 'My father should have sent for me before now.'

She spoke the words almost painfully. Before she had laid eyes on young Archibald Douglas? That might have left her heart-whole. Now it was too late. Now she was less than strong because her mind and passions were filled with thoughts of him. It was less than sensible but she could do no other. She had lost her heart to him.

* * *

A packman arrived a few days later to say that he had heard it from another, recently travelled from the Border, that a great army was now mustered near Twizel Bridge on the Till and that the Earl of Surrey was leading the English troops. Such men often embroidered their tales to make a good story in the hopes of extra bounty, but this man had a fearful look in his eyes.

'They are marching on to Flodden Hill,' the packman was telling John Dykes when Sarah came upon them in the kitchen quarters.

'I heard from Grey Tammas that he listened to a great soldier telling another that the English halberds would soon destroy the pikes. They are not so long, you see, and are manageable at close quarters.'

Sarah shivered. Why must men always think of themselves as soldiers willing to kill one another with these terrible weapons? She could use a sword herself and would not be slow with a dagger to defend herself, but this killing in battle was more than she could stomach at times.

Her father would be there with the King.

And what about Douglas? His father was there, and his uncle, as she knew. He was making plans to join them after he left the Queen's service. Suppose he were pierced by an arrow, or an English bill?

Sarah's face drained of colour and she felt sick as she bade John Dykes reward the packman for his news, and buy in some of his wares. They would receive more news of battles being fought soon enough by messenger, but the packman had his own way of finding out what was happening. It was a great asset to their trade.

* * *

Two days later one of their own servants rode in, his horse lathering as he brought news from the battlefield. He had heard the messenger who rode into Edinburgh in all his armour of battle to tell the presidents of the capital city that the battle was a victory for Surrey. Beyond that he could not tell, or hesitated to tell his young mistress.

'But ... but where is the King?' she demanded.

'I know not, Mistress Sarah,' he told her.

'And my ... my father?'

The servant, still only a boy, shook his head.

'No, Mistress, nor news of any other.'

'What of Douglas?' she wanted to cry. 'What of that nobleman?'

But there was only an ominous silence from the south-east of Larraig, well south of Edinburgh and towards the Borders.

Sarah drew on every ounce of courage and went to pacify her grandmother who was thumping the floor for attention with a heavy stick. The child, Jamie, was asleep, worn out with his play.

CHAPTER THREE

Sir Thomas rode home two days later, his head wrapped in bandages and his weakened body supported by Robin Drummond, younger son of Sir Neil Drummond.

Robin was a slender young man, very little taller than Sarah, and with a lazy, slightly affected manner learned, no doubt, during the years he had spent in France serving King Louis XII. His slender elegant hands looked as though they might be more at home with his pen than his sword.

His older brother, Archibald, was nearly twice his size and no one cared to quarrel with him. He was very like his father, but Sir Neil had lost an arm at Sauchieburn and had handed on his sword to Archibald.

Sarah's eyes flickered when she saw that it was Robin who had brought her father home. For the briefest moment she had mistaken him for Archibald, having recognized the party as being the Drummonds of Balwhidden. If she had not fallen in love with Douglas, she might have been looking out eagerly for Archibald Drummond whom she admired a great deal, but she had no special admiration for Robin who, she had long decided, was more of a girl than a man with his fair cheeks and slender hands.

His elegant body was displayed to best advantage dancing a reel rather than putting on armour. It was no surprise to her now that Robin showed no sign of wounds from battle, though the few men who accompanied them were already half falling out of the saddle and were being helped into the Great Hall. It only surprised her that Robin had gone to fight for his King at all, and had not found it expedient to return to France!

'John Dykes, and whatever men you have left are needed here,' he said gently to Sarah. 'Your father had his head battered for him, but he will be better in time. We need to look at the wound.'

'Father!'

Sarah rushed forward and would have taken him in her arms, but Sir Thomas shook his head feebly even as Robin Drummond held out a hand.

'He is well enough and you cannot help him at this stage. I have left word for the surgeon to travel to Larraig and Balwhidden where my brother also needs attention.'

The din was incredible, between the howling of the dogs, the clatter of horses and the shouts of men in pain from their wounds, but she could hear every word spoken in his low voice.

'It is indeed fortunate that you, yourself, are unscathed, sir,' she said and for a moment their eyes met.

He was as dark as she was fair, but his eyes were a piercing blue and for a brief moment they sparkled with anger. Then he bowed politely and smiled.

'Why, Mistress Sarah,' he said, pleasantly, 'I had not thought to see you such a fine lady. Truly your months at Court have not improved your manners.'

It was Sarah's turn to flush and she was about to make a scathing reply when the men hurried forward to help Sir Thomas and carry him indoors where Lady Margaret was commanding the maidservants to prepare beds. Her rheumatism had improved miraculously and she hobbled about with great energy and competence. Jamie was in the care of one of the servants, as he looked on with wide eyes and a flush on his soft cheeks. His father was a great warrior. He, too, would be a great warrior one day.

* * *

Sir Thomas was put to bed and the women

brought in from neighbouring farms to help dress the wounded, then beds were found so that they could be rested and fed. It was many weary hours before Sarah could draw breath and take stock of herself, and Larraig.

Robin Drummond was given quarters on the orders of Sir Thomas, who seemed to cling closely to the younger man, and with greater intensity than Sarah would have supposed. At one time he had had no great opinion of Balwhidden's younger son, and now this new attitude alarmed her quite a lot. Had the wound on her father's head addled his mind? Why should he embrace Robin so fervently?

She learned that Sir Thomas believed Robin Drummond had saved his life, but by the younger man's own admission, he had stayed on the outskirts of the battle and 'observed for future enlightenment', as he put it delicately, with a raised eyebrow.

'Whilst our men were falling around you?' she asked, scathingly.

Again the blue sparks darted from his eyes.

'It was a misjudged battle, Mistress Sarah, and to rush at the enemy offering to bare one's breast to their axes in a useless cause is not my idea of bravery. More battles are won with brains than with brawn, and I think you will agree that I am lacking a little of the latter quality.'

Sarah said nothing, but her looks spoke for her and Drummond sighed and stretched out an elegant leg.

Lady Margaret had gone to bed, and Sarah had come to sit with Drummond in front of the fire in the lesser hall whilst the servants cleared up after the meal. She had wanted to hear everything which had happened though her heart was heavy as she saw the dull defeated looks on the faces of the men who had survived a great disaster if she had wit enough to read the facts aright.

'So you must hear all,' Robin said with a twisted smile. 'Very well, you shall hear it. It was after four o'clock on the ninth September when we met the enemy and we roared our cannon at them, and they roared theirs back at us, but to my mind it makes more noise than anything else.

'We were in a fine position at Flodden Hill and Surrey was trying to get us down on to the plain, but the King refused to move, and rightly at first.

'Then Surrey began to circle round us and my own commander, Huntly, would have had the King make his move then, but he would not. He was listening to that Englishman, Musgrave, so he bided where he was. Then when they saw that Surrey was about to cut us off from the rest of our kingdom, with their army spread out as it was, Musgrave must advise the King to move, and move we did ... into Hell!'

His eyes had grown as hard as sapphires as

23

he gazed into the fire.

'We did well with Lord Home's division and scattered the English right wing, but Lennox and Argyle could not suffer the arrows and broke ranks. They rushed downhill and could not be stopped, except by the English under Stanley. Maybe we should have given them more help, but they would not be brought to discipline.'

'And ... and the King?' Sarah asked, fearfully.

Robin shook his head. 'There is much I do not know. He had the great nobles with him, in good armour, though some say on foot. Our pikes are no match for those bills. They make fearful wounds. At first it seemed that we would win the day, then we were given orders to retire. My brother is wounded, but not mortally. He has men enough to see him home, so that I came with your father whose head received a dunt like to fell a lesser man. There ... there are rumours that the King is dead, though some say he was captured by four horsemen and was seen crossing the Tweed in their midst at nightfall. We will know the truth soon enough.'

There was deep silence between them. Sarah wanted desperately to ask about Douglas, but a tentative question told her that Robin Drummond knew no more than he was telling her, or if he did know, he preferred to keep that knowledge to himself.

Again, there had been a knowing look in his eyes when she singled the name out of all others. Her voice had trembled and she had seen him go still as a cat before he took his time to reply.

'A chamber has been prepared for you, sir,' she said, politely, having gained no more news. 'My father asks that you be our guest for as long as you wish.'

'I thank him for his hospitality,' Drummond told her, 'but I will leave Larraig in another hour. I will take two of my men.'

'But you cannot!' she protested. Now that she looked at him closely, having watched him shed his outer garments, and helmet, she saw how white and tired he looked. Something stirred in her heart. He had been an adolescent boy when she was still a child and he had always been kind to her where Archibald had sometimes teased her cruelly, holding her aloft in his great strong arms and laughing when she grew afraid. She had hated Archibald in those days, for his lack of feeling, but Robin had always stood up to his brother, forcing him to put her down and allow her to play in her own fashion.

Archibald would laugh. 'Lassie-boy', he would taunt, and encourage Sarah to laugh with him, whilst the soft pink colour stained Robin's smooth delicate cheeks.

Earl Drummond, himself, had sent Robin to Paris to be educated and later he served at the

French Court. He could write in Greek, Latin and French with equal ease, but he was certainly no warrior and had not the strength of his brother or others like him.

'You cannot go until you are rested, Robin,' Sarah told him, more gently. 'Balwhidden can wait. I know Sir Neil and Lady Elspeth will be waiting to see you, but they will be busy with Archibald and his men. You have already sent the surgeon there and can do no more. Rest here a day or two.'

'I will rest by the fire and...' he poked the fire with his foot, '... I do not return to Balwhidden. I ... I have other things to do.'

'What things?'

'Shall we say they are of a private nature?' he asked, gently.

She flushed. Of course he must have a woman waiting to hear that he was well. Yet she had never heard of a woman in his life. There had been much fun-poking and laughs behind the hand that young Drummond was more the woman himself than one likely to impress a young lady with his strong manhood. Sarah had tried to pretend that she did not understand such talk, but now she looked at him more intently, her eyes roving over his face.

It was an unusual face, pale-skinned and with delicate bones. His hair was very black and fell in soft curls about his broad white forehead. His chin was strong and firm, however, and Sarah decided that it was not a weak face. He was as nothing for handsome looks compared with Douglas or even his older brother, but he was certainly not ill-looking.

'Well?' Robin asked, 'are you thinking I might well fall off my horse with fatigue? I assure you that I have learned the trick of resting in the saddle. I will not take any hurt, but it warms my heart that you show such concern for me.'

His tone was mocking and there was a hint of laughter in his blue eyes. Again she flushed rosily and rather angrily. He was so quick to attribute one with motives one did not possess.

'Will you see my father before you ride out, sir, otherwise he will be aggrieved that we allowed you to go with so little rest?'

'Aye, that I promise. I will see him in another hour.'

* * *

Sarah was shut out of the interview between Drummond and her father, then the younger man slipped quietly out of Larraig before dawn rose up from the east, and the mists rose like clouds on the mountains until the sun dispersed them with the warmth of a new day.

CHAPTER FOUR

Sarah had no time to speculate about Drummond's destination because John Dykes came to find her and to inform her that the surgeon was waiting in the Great Hall and would attend Sir Thomas, having moved on from Balwhidden.

'I will come at once,' Sarah informed him. She had wrapped herself in a shawl and rested a while after Robin Drummond rode out, and now she tidied her hair and put on her blue woollen over-gown. Her best silks and velvets were hung away in a special cupboard designed to keep the moths at bay.

Clattering down the stone stairs, she hurried to meet the surgeon, an elderly man with a grizzled beard, faded velvet cap and a long brown home-spun coat over his grey linen shirt.

'Ewan Armour at your service, Madam,' he greeted her.

'You are welcome, Ewan Armour,' she told him politely. 'Have you broken your fast?'

'No, Madam. I had escort from Balwhidden, but we left in the small hours for ease of travel. There are small parties of men returning home from the battle and ... and I cannot serve everybody, Madam, or I could not live.'

'That is understood,' said Sarah, quickly.

She did not care very much for Ewan Armour, but she gave instructions immediately that he, and the escort from Balwhidden, should be served with good meat. Ewan Armour would stay at Larraig until Sir Thomas's wounds improved.

'How fares the Earl of Balwhidden?' she asked.

'Well enough, and Sir Archibald though he has a bad wound on the lower part of his body and has lost blood, but nothing that a strong man cannot stand. It is the older men, like Sir Thomas Graham, who are very sick of their wounds. They go out to the wars thinking themselves young again, but old bones are harder to mend.'

'I will take you to my father as soon as you have satisfied your hunger,' said Sarah. 'Did you meet Master Robin Drummond on his way back to Balwhidden?'

'That I did not, Madam, but he may have taken a different route.'

He was eyeing her curiously and Sarah blushed with annoyance. She had no real interest in Robin Drummond.

'When you are ready then,' she said, impatiently, and the man pushed back his empty plate, having drained his tankard of light ale.

Ewan Armour rose to his feet, having divested himself of his outer garments, and put on a clean linen over-shirt. Suddenly he was a different man, full of confidence and with a brisk and businesslike manner.

'I need warm water and certain herbs which I carry in my baggage. If a maidservant can bring me the water, and bowls for me to mix the herbs, we can be on our way. Is there a woman who will nurse Sir Thomas?'

'Anna Hyslop,' said Sarah. 'She is with him now.'

'Will she be able to supply clean linen, Madam?'

'It shall be supplied,' Sarah told him, 'and I shall help you as well as Anna.'

'You are only a young maiden, if I must be plain, Madam. Leave such a task to the nurse woman.'

'I want to see how badly my father is wounded. Apart from my grandmother and young brother, he is all I have and I care for him. Besides, you should know that we learn quickly how to heal wounds, we who remain at home.'

'Aye, but the patient will not wish to show weakness before his daughter.'

'Then he should not have gone to fight,' said Sarah, crisply.

She had listened so often to Queen Margaret who had said there was no need for this war, and Sarah was beginning to feel that her life was changing against her will and she could do little about it. If only she could see Douglas again. It seemed a long time since she had last looked into his appraising eyes. He had admired her, she thought, remembering those bold eyes weighing her up. They might have become friends if they had been given more time. As soon as her father was back to good health and her grandmother remained in reasonable health, also, she would ask to be allowed to go back to Court. She pushed aside the thought that her grandmother was now too frail to be left.

But would the Court remain the same? wondered Sarah, with sudden shock almost like a douche of cold water. What if the King was badly wounded? Had he been captured, and, perhaps, held to ransom? The Queen would be sovereign until he was returned to Edinburgh once more, and the Court be it at Edinburgh or Stirling, would be full of her advisers. The Douglases and the Hamiltons would jostle each other for power, and the Court, too, would be changed.

Sarah felt inordinately irritated and at odds with herself as she conducted Ewan Armour to Sir Thomas's chamber. Robin Drummond had upset her but she hardly knew why. There had been battles fought in the past and both sides had ridden away to lick their wounds before gathering themselves together for another quarrel. Scotland had always quarrelled with England, even as England quarrelled with France.

But this was different, thought Sarah. This

battle had been a great deal more serious. She had sensed that knowledge in Robin Drummond and now in her father as he lay in his bed and stared with fevered eyes at the surgeon.

'So you will mend me, sir?' he asked. 'To what use? I am over the age for this task.'

'I do not have to make it plain then,' Ewan Armour agreed. 'Come, let me see the wounds.'

'Not until my daughter leaves my chamber. This is not for your eyes, Sarah.'

'I am a woman now, Father. If I can keep the castle, I can dress a wound.'

'Not for your father. Let the surgeon and Anna do their worst.'

The old nursemaid now came to take the girl's hands. She had nursed Mistress Sarah when she was a baby and was like a mother to her.

'Go rest yourself,' she said, and the girl nodded, after she and Anna measured one another. Her fatigue was beginning to show.

'I will lie down for an hour or two.'

But the cry of pain which burst from Sir Thomas's lips when the surgeon pulled the dirty bandage from his head was echoed throughout Larraig, and Sarah lay on her bed and suffered with him.

'Please, God, relieve his pain,' she prayed, and 'please God, do not let Douglas lie wounded on the field, or in a sick-bed.'

It would be terrible to have such wounds on such a fine body.

*　　*　　*

The days passed in a haze of noise, activity, fatigue and a nameless apprehension which refused to go away even when Sir Thomas began to show improvement in his health. The fever which drove him into delirium so that he could be heard shouting his instructions to his men through his pain, and requiring to be soothed with cooling linen cloths wrung out in herbal water, wrought in him fiercely.

Sarah insisted on being present in the sickroom despite her grandmother's protests being added to those of Anna Hyslop, and when the fever died out of Sir Thomas's wild eyes, he would order her feebly from the room.

'I am needed here, Father,' she protested. 'Grandmother has regained the use of her legs with her temper and her tongue. She guards the household. You forget that I am truly a woman now and no longer a mere child.'

'I do not forget,' Sir Thomas growled as he began to feel better. 'We will talk about that as soon as I have strength to sit up in my bed. My head got a fearful dunt. I have never known such a headache and I am lucky to have my sight. It was an axe which near cleaved me in two.'

'It makes me shiver to hear you tell the tale,' Sarah said and again apprehension grew in her.

What if her father had been killed? How would she have fared, trying to keep Larraig for her brother?

And what about the King? And the baby, Prince Jamie? Who would help Queen Margaret if the King had, indeed, been killed? She would need help to govern the kingdom and there were still powerful noblemen waiting to grab power into their own hands. Not all of them had fallen at Flodden.

Women tried very hard to be strong, but no woman was a match for a man like the Earl of Arran who was the King's uncle, by marriage, or even the Earl of Angus, head of the House of Douglas. If Angus got power, then his grandson would be even further beyond her reach, thought Sarah, as she tidied the sick-room whilst her father lay snoring, then began to mutter uneasily in his sleep. His mind was greatly disturbed, thought Sarah, looking down on him. He had grown suddenly older and his straw-coloured hair was fading to white. At the moment he had less strength in him than his own mother.

'Helen,' he muttered, 'Helen...'

Sarah's heart lurched then ached, knowing that he still clung in his heart to his dead wife.

'Hush, Father,' she said, softly, and began to wipe his forehead again. Anna Hyslop had been dozing by the fireside but now she woke, startled, and the movement also brought Sir Thomas to his senses.

'Is he ridden in yet?' he asked, anxiously.

'Who, Father? The surgeon? He has gone on to Edinburgh where he has been called to help. There are many wounded waiting his services. We will see to you, Father.'

'I talk about Robin Drummond,' Sir Thomas said, impatiently. 'I wish to see him at once, as soon as he rides in.'

Sarah stared at him nonplussed. What should she tell him? That Drummond had been at Larraig and had now ridden away? Drummond would be returning to Balwhidden after he had attended to his own private business. He had fulfilled his obligations to the Grahams. There was no need for him to do more.

Larraig was lucky to lose fewer men than most in this battle, Sarah knew. Her father would recover as would several of his men though there was great grieving in some of the cottages. She would need to ride out to offer comfort and see who might require to be taken into Larraig. If the man of the house was killed, his widow and children were vulnerable and might starve unless she were a strong woman with growing sons, able to dig their plot.

Sarah hoped her father would gather his strength soon. Larraig was not large, but it was too much for her to manage, even if her grandmother was strong enough to hector the servants, which she did frequently. She hobbled around on an old stick and was not averse to laying it across the backs of the lazier servants.

'Meat has to be earned,' she would say, fiercely, 'and rest. We were given arms for hard work, and legs to walk on. And your backside is for kicking if ye sit on it too much.'

Yet she had a knack of watching to see if any of the servants were sick, or weak through bad health, and here she would be infinitely patient and gentle.

'They cannot work if their bodies are in poor health,' she would tell Sarah, 'we must strengthen the bodies up again.'

Some preferred to work rather than face Lady Margaret's remedies for the good of their health, potions which she encouraged Anna Hyslop to brew for her. They were mainly derived from dandelions and nettles. She was convinced that God grew remedies for all ills, within a stone's throw of a cotter's doorstep, if only they would take the trouble to look.

Now she was brewing up broth for Sir Thomas which, she claimed, would soon have him back on his feet.

'He is very restless,' said Sarah, coming to find her grandmother. 'The poisons are still going through his body. The English weapons would be dirty most likely.'

'Aye. As I have often told you, my lass, 'tis dirt which poisons the blood. I have seen it afore many times.'

'Grandmother ... is there any more news? Has ... has anybody been here with news whilst I was with my father?'

'Narry a body,' said Lady Margaret, shaking her head. 'It is quiet, Sarah, too quiet for my liking. I do not like the feeling. There is no doubt we have taken the worst of it all from what I hear, and our men are limping home except for the thousands left on the field. And, thousands was what one of our own men told me. And they say the Border towns are cut off, and that is bad. That is very bad. We will have to gird ourselves, my dear lass. The Earl o' Surrey is only drawing breath and I expect he will be following up his advantage.'

'Marching north, you mean?' asked Sarah, her eyes wide as this thought struck her.

'Would you not expect him to do that? He is no fool, that same gentleman, the great Surrey. I met him years ago when he brought the young Queen to marry the King... not so many years, though it seems a lifetime. But what an occasion that was! You were a child then, Sarah, but we all went, including Thomas and Helen, and there was great jousting in the streets and many a sore head at the end of the day.'

She was silent for a while, shaking her head at the memory.

'The Queen's brother, Henry, is a different man from his father, Henry the Seventh. The old King never went to war if he could help it, but this younger Henry ... now ... he's a different man, Sarah. If you ask me, he likes warring and battles and fighting, and I have a notion that our own King James, God bless him, is not far behind him. They do not mind insulting one another ... only ... only their loyal servants have to give their lives for their quarrels, and from what we fear, King James might have quarrelled once too often. I fear the news, Sarah.'

'But surely those quarrels are justified, Grandmother.'

'Some of them, of course, and that on both sides. But now we maybe have to pay for losing this battle. We must be prepared, my lass, for what might come and we must make plans for provisions to be stored in places other than our normal stores, also for animals to be brought in from the fields. We must prepare for a long winter with fuel and salted meats and fish.'

'What if we are put to the torch, Grandmother?' Sarah asked, fearfully.

She had been burned accidentally as a child, and now dreaded fire more than any other hazard.

'We will see, child, we will see. We need your father's health to be restored, and to have him well and strong. We do not have enough strong men at Larraig since the child is so young. God grant that our good King is safe somewhere and it is not as we fear. His heir is still a poor babe and it has happened so too often in our history. The Stewarts are a reckless family, Sarah, but they are God's anointed. They are set apart, even from the nobles.'

Sarah nodded and her heart felt cold when she thought about the King. Surely there would be news by now, if he were being held for ransom. News of that order would spread like wildfire.

'Do you remember the tale about the man in the blue robe?' she asked Lady Margaret.

The old woman looked into the girl's anxious face.

'They were only tales, child. Others were told at the same time, tales which no doubt filled a packman's belly or a drover's.'

'But that man entreated the King not to go gathering an army for war, whilst the King was at his devotions, or so they say.'

'Well, if the King paid no attention, I do not think we should be anxious. James saw and spoke to this man, and we did not. We can only listen to rumours and fairy stories.'

Nevertheless the old woman's eyes held a hint of fear as she finished her chores and set her brewed herbs aside until they could be bottled and labelled. She was an old woman with her life behind her, but Sarah was young and beautiful beyond belief. She could see the stamp of great beauty on the child's face and form. But it was best to keep her busy, and her silks and satins hung away in the closet near the privy to keep the moths away.

Sarah had blossomed out even in these past few weeks, and it was expedient for them to keep her away from that young rogue, Douglas. He would soon notice her if she returned to Court and he would have no intention of behaving honourably towards Larraig. Mistress Sarah Graham would be of no consequence to the great Angus. Nothing short of royalty for them.

No, it was best to keep Sarah away.

CHAPTER FIVE

Sarah was scarcely conscious of the weeks passing after Flodden, but it was long enough before Sir Thomas was well enough to sit up in his bed and to ask Sarah to come and sit with him because he had a wish to talk to her about her future.

Sarah had been busy helping with the wounded, finding clean linen for bandages at the behest of Lady Margaret who thought that there was healing power in bright spring water.

'Man is baptized in the name of the Lord with water,' she said. 'That means that evil spirits are driven from the body by water and we must use it to drive out impurities from wounds. Cleanse all the linen with water, Sarah. That is how we will make our wounded well again, whilst others perish with sickness.'

The remedy had been used to good effect on Sir Thomas and now he sat up in bed and argued with Anna Hyslop over drinking her broth when a stronger brew, he claimed, would have done him more good.

'You are as weak as a babe, Maister,' the old woman told him, 'so I will feed you like a babe. Drink this good broth made with fine beef. It will put strength into your limbs. You will have the young ladies admiring again in no time and you can be thinking about another wife.'

'None of your coquetry,' he told her as her eyes rolled to the ceiling. 'You are a bad lass, Anna Hyslop.'

'Well, I am not a done-up babe yet myself and you are younger than I am,' she retorted.

'Go and cool yourself down, woman,' he advised, 'and send Mistress Sarah to me. It is time I talked with her.'

Sarah wore a clean linen over-dress and cap when she went to see her father and he frowned when he saw her.

'You dress like the maidservants,' he complained. 'Where are your Court gowns?'

'They were not suitable for Larraig, Father. Here I must help with the household.'

'Your grandmother can command help. You must not forget that you are my daughter. My daughter is not a servant in my household.'

Sarah bit back a sharp retort. Was her father not aware that by going off to war with the best of their men, they had diminished household help? The women servants were kept busy attending the sick and the men were preparing

Larraig against siege, should the Earl of Surrey decide to follow up his victory.

'Have you no word from Robbie?' he asked.

'Robin Drummond?' She raised an eyebrow. 'He rode out some days ago and has not been back since. I would have supposed he returned to Balwhidden.'

'He is returning to Larraig when he has accomplished what he has set out to do. I have arranged that he stays here as my squire until I am well enough to take my proper place again. He is a younger son and is happy to agree to that request. It will be years before Jamie is fitted to run Larraig.'

'You forget that I am here, Father.'

Spots of colour burned in Sarah's cheeks. 'It is the Queen who helps to guard our realm whilst the King goes off to battle, and it is the women of our kingdom who have to learn to manage the land and make decisions like the men. My grandmother still makes those decisions for us.'

'She is grown old and I do not wish you to take on this responsibility when it can be done by a man.'

She stared at him. 'You ... you mean Robin Drummond?'

'Who else? I have negotiated with him, and Sir Neil, that there should be a marriage between the two of you, and he is willing to take you for his wife. It should be a good arrangement...'

'Father!'

She could scarcely speak and the word was almost a whisper as she interrupted him.

'Father... you cannot mean what you say! Maybe... maybe Robin Drummond *is* willing, but I am not!'

Sir Thomas stared at her. 'You see, it is not a good idea to allow you to manage Larraig. It begins to put a man's head on a maid's shoulders, and you feel you can defy your father, and question his intentions. I know what is best for my own daughter, and that is Robbie. Oh, I know there are those who say he is not a big strong man, but it is my belief that a good strong heart beats within his slender frame, and that is what counts, my daughter. I could have offered you to a man a great many years older who would not be a good companion for you.'

'Are there any such men left?' she asked, almost wildly, 'with the news that is coming up from the south? It surprises me that we have any of our good *brave* men left.'

She emphasized the word to show what she thought of Robin Drummond.

'You have said enough,' Sir Thomas told her and leaned back wearily. Her heart was suddenly stirred when she saw his white face, but her anger was also great. How could he suggest such a thing? She did not love Robin Drummond, but she knew that if she said so, Sir Thomas would not listen.

'Send Robbie to me as soon as he returns.'

'Am I permitted to ask where he has gone?'

'He had an errand for Queen Margaret. That is all I can tell you. She will be Queen Regent if ... if the King truly *is* dead, but it was not certain what happened at Flodden. He may be held by Surrey for ransom.'

'My Lord Douglas will surely serve the Queen,' she ventured, diffidently, the colour gradually staining her cheeks. She could *not* marry Drummond. Even if Douglas was not for her, she could not so readily tear him from her heart. She loved him, so how could she learn to love Drummond? Her father and mother had scarcely met when they were married, but they had fallen passionately in love with one another, and Sir Thomas thought that this could happen to everyone, if the match was 'suitable'.

Now Sarah felt sick at heart when she thought about the handsome young man whose eyes had followed her admiringly when they were at Court. In her imagination she had built up every glance, every smile, into something of importance between them and she hugged those memories close to her heart. They filled her dreams with warmth and excitement. Such love as she was beginning to feel for Douglas must surely be returned. Yet how could she nurture that love if she pledged it, before God, to another man?

Sir Thomas was regarding her closely and

Sarah turned away and stared out beyond the narrow window as though to will a happening which would save her from being obliged to obey her father in this and every matter. She was his daughter and he had full power over her.

'I had expected to return to Court to resume my duties in helping to nurse Prince Jamie.'

'He may be Prince no longer,' Sir Thomas sighed. 'It happens too often in our history that the heir to our throne is still a babe. There will be a great struggle for power, you will see. I know what old Angus plans, if the King is killed in battle. He plans to marry that grandson of his to the Queen Regent, and to gain control of the boy King.'

Sarah's face lost all colour.

'I do not believe it!' she cried in a ringing voice.

Her father's brows went black as he stared at her, his slight fever giving his face a sterner look than usual.

'It seems to me, Mistress, that it is time you were married and under a husband's control. Truly my mother has been lax with you, and it would not have happened if your mother were alive. She would teach you better manners.'

Her anger and distress had brought defiance to her and Sir Thomas knew fear when he looked at her beauty. It was not wise to allow this daughter to go to Court. There were those who would despoil a young woman, however well-born, and there was going to be a great thirst for power between the two most powerful families, the Douglases of Angus and the Hamiltons of Arran.

The Earl of Arran was the King's uncle by marriage, having married the sister of James III, and now Angus was planning to wed his grandson to Queen Margaret, should she now be widowed. A young comely woman, such as she was, with full powers in her hands as mother of the new King, could not remain in that state for long. Thomas had sat in on a very private meeting one evening after Angus and several of the other powerful barons had failed to persuade the King against going to war with England. His people would fight for him, as they all knew, because he was beloved by all, but it was madness to weaken the kingdom in this way at this time, when the quarrel was not great. Nor would the King accept that he could be killed in battle.

'I leave my crown to my son,' he said, impatiently, 'and the kingdom in the care of my wife, Queen Margaret, until he comes of age, though why trouble ourselves with matters which will not happen? I am a match for any general who dares to set foot in my kingdom, or who insults our ally, France.'

'The man in the blue gown,' someone had muttered, and the King's face suffused with colour.

'Who is weak-kneed about a poor madman?

I let him go because he was deranged, but I might not be so generous with those who pay attention to his senseless ramblings.'

Later Angus had gathered his own around him and had put his fears into words, unaware that other ears could hear as well as those of his two sons.

'The Queen will need help and advice if the King does not heed that man in the azure-blue,' he said, 'whether he be madman or ... or as we all fear ... Saint John, sent by the Virgin Mary as a warning to be heeded. We must be prepared. The child king must not be brought up by the Hamiltons.'

Sir Thomas had listened and knew, with great anguish, that the kingdom was likely to be split in two if King James was killed in battle. There would be quarrelling amongst the greater barons and when that happened, the whole kingdom was at its most vulnerable.

And he was not at all sure that he favoured either Douglas, Earl of Angus, or Hamilton, Earl of Arran. Neither of them could command love and loyalty such as that bestowed by the people on King James.

And perhaps that love and loyalty would be the death of him, Sir Thomas had thought, shivering. Without it he could not hope to gather the army round him which he would need if he were to challenge King Henry of England. Henry, too, had not the calm breadth of vision of his father, Henry VII, and he had already insulted their own King by declaring him negligible. James was hot-blooded to prove himself the better man.

They had gone to war, Sir Thomas now mused, and to disaster, and now Robbie Drummond was carrying a message from the Queen to her brother. Sir Thomas hoped that King Henry would be wise enough to see that he could not subdue his northern neighbour by invasion and even conquering the country. Robin would be carrying that message privately as between brother and sister and Sir Thomas prayed that it would be heeded. If it was not heeded, then the barons would never stop fighting. Henry might win a few battles, but he would never win the kingdom and there would never be peace in the land.

Sir Thomas grew tired. He was old at heart despite Anna Hyslop's words. She was an old sinner, he thought, fondly. She would have a young female in his bed little older than his own daughter. Well, he was too tired for such ploys, but there were a few years ahead before Jamie was old enough to look after Larraig. Robin Drummond would make a fine job of managing the estate. He could marry Sarah, if she would get that nonsense about young Douglas out of her head. She must think him a simpleton not to read the signs that she had fallen in love with the man. Yet no man in the kingdom could be more unsuitable for Sarah than the grandson of Angus. They were seeking the greatest in the land for him, as Thomas knew very well.

'I will not have nonsense from you, Mistress,' he said, harshly. 'You should be down on your knees with gratitude that I have found you such a fine man in Robbie.'

A fine man! thought Sarah. Where were her father's eyes? Why, Robin Drummond was more the woman than the man. He was as graceful as a girl, though perhaps that was why the Queen had chosen him to do her errands. He could ride like the wind, being no doubt as light as a feather on his horse.

But she wanted a *man*, not a mere boy as pretty as Robin. Besides, he had never shown signs of being attracted to her. Instead he often behaved like a mountebank.

'Does Robin Drummond support the match?' she asked. 'Is it what *he* wants, or does he wish to please you and his own father?'

'I talked this over with his father, the earl. He likes it well enough. His brother will inherit Balwhidden and is already promised in marriage. Robbie can take an interest in Larraig, with you by his side.'

'So he has to do what his father bids,' said Sarah, rather bitterly.

It was exactly what she had suspected. She was being handed over to Robin who did not even want her!

'Send Anna Hyslop to me,' Sir Thomas told her, wearily. 'It is time I rested. I have told your grandmother my wishes and she agrees that I am doing the best possible thing for you. Is Jamie at his lessons?'

'Yes, sir, he is, though he is young for study.'

Jamie was only a baby, thought Sarah, yet her father and grandmother would have him a man before his time. He was learning Latin, Greek and French already with the monks, and in her opinion he would have been better employed playing football.

Sarah checked her own thoughts. Grandmother had said she would make a milksop out of Jamie if she tried to protect him, and perhaps this was so. She would have enough of milksops if she married Robin Drummond!

CHAPTER SIX

Robin rode in ten days later looking wearied to death, though only the tell-tale signs of his white face and dark-ringed eyes showed that weariness to Sir Thomas. For Sarah he had nothing but inane laughter and small talk.

'Why, Mistress Sarah, were you watching for me?' he asked and blue lights twinkled in his eyes. 'I see you are rushing to greet me as soon as I ride in.'

'That is not so,' she said, angrily. 'I mean I was *not* watching for you. It is merely by accident that I am here, in the courtyard, just when you arrive.'

'Well, no matter. The result is the same and I declare myself glad to be back in Larraig. I hope Sir Thomas is well, and can receive me.'

'He is improving in health, and has given orders that he will receive you as soon as you arrive. Will you have refreshment first, sir?'

Her tone was carefully polite and she avoided looking at him as much as possible. She could not yet believe that her father had promised her to this man.

'I ate meat at Balwhidden, and I ride a fresh horse. I would prefer to see Sir Thomas now.'

'Very well, if you will come with me, I will take you to him,' she said quietly, but with all the dignity proper to a lady.

What hold must Robin Drummond have over her father? wondered Sarah, as she conducted the young man to Sir Thomas's chamber. The older man had been fractious and ill-tempered for the past few days, now that his head was beginning to heal. He was still too weak to go about his affairs, as he had found out after defying Anna Hyslop, who raged at him noisily as he swung himself on to his feet and tried to rise. The result had been a fresh pouring of blood from the wound, and disappointment which had gone ill with his temper. Now he greeted Robbie as though the younger man were, indeed, his own son.

'You are tired, my boy. Have ye rested?' he

asked after grasping his hands in his own, and looking closely into his face.

'Long enough, sir. I knew you would want to hear all the news, so I came as fast as I could.'

'And?'

'Not good, but better in some ways. Alas, sir, our good King James is dead.'

There was silence for a while as both men fought their emotions and Sarah's eyes filled with tears. The whole kingdom would mourn for him, she knew, and immediately her thoughts were with Queen Margaret. How sad for her to be widowed while she was still a young woman.

And the poor babe, Prince Jamie! He would now be King, and he was not yet two years old.

'Long live King James the Fifth of Scotland,' Sir Thomas murmured.

'Long live King James the Fifth,' Robin Drummond echoed, 'I have already pledged my loyalty and allegiance to him.'

'Tell us what you know about the death of the King,' Sir Thomas commanded. 'Tell me all about the battle, lad, as though I had not been there for, in truth, my head has blanked out most of it for me after receiving this blow from an English axe.'

Robin nodded rather wearily.

'Well, sir, as you know we were doing well under Home and Huntly on the left wing and had them routed, and there are those who are accusing Home and saying he should have pressed home his advantage and gone to help the King. But the English, under Sir Edmund Howard got reinforcements from Dacre and we were obliged to defend ourselves again. That was when you got the crack on the head.'

'Aye, aye,' Sir Thomas said, impatiently. 'What about the rest of it?'

'The right wing under Lennox and Argyle had to break ranks because the Highlanders such as McLean and MacKenzie found themselves showered by English arrows and rushed to attack. The English under Sir Edward Stanley commanded the Lancashire and Cheshire Regiments and ... and they lost the day. There...' Robin glanced at Sarah who was listening intently, '... there was great slaughter, sir.'

Sir Thomas was silent for a while.

'And the King?' he asked, finally.

'Stood his ground with the greatest of our earls around him. They fought Surrey and did well under Bothwell, but the English advanced on all sides. By nightfall they found that the King had been killed, and the heart went out of the battle for us. The army withdrew and rumours abounded over what had happened to the King, but the truth is that Lord Dacre found the King's body and took it to Berwick where it has been presented to Surrey. It was identified by Sir Walter Scott and Sir John Forman. They were two of the King's closest attendants and knew very well that the body they saw was that of King James. Queen Margaret has been informed. She is at Stirling, and our new King has been crowned there. Long live the King.'

'Long live the King,' Sir Thomas and Sarah repeated once again, fervently, though each felt sick and empty at the thought of the loss to their kingdom of their dearly loved James IV. His energy and imagination had brought new prosperity to their land, but that same leadership had also decimated the land, as they well knew.

If only she could go to Stirling *now*, thought Sarah, and help the Queen. Lady Jane Hamilton would need help in looking after the baby King, and how much happier this would be for her than marriage with Robin Drummond.

She looked at him with new eyes as he lounged wearily in a chair beside her father's bed.

'And does Surrey prepare for war anew?' Sir Thomas was asking.

'The Presidents of Edinburgh have given orders for a great wall to be built around the city. The Provost and Magistrates have perished in the battle, but the Presidents are taking command and have brought order out of confusion to the city. For reasons I cannot discuss...' again he looked at Sarah, '... I do not think King Henry will try to invade our realm.'

Robin Drummond did not wish to discuss the private message he had taken from Queen Margaret to her brother's Court in England. He had scarcely slept until his task was accomplished, and now he felt weary to death.

He turned eyes which flamed with extreme fatigue towards Sarah and suddenly her heart was touched. She would have felt the same compassion for any man, she assured herself.

'Say no more, sir,' she told him. 'If you will come along to your bedchamber, you will find everything ready for you to rest. It has been waiting for several days and John Dykes will have ordered everything to be made as you would wish. Food will be served.'

'No food, as I say. But I will be happy to rest.'

She nodded and conducted him to the chamber after he had taken leave of Sir Thomas.

'We will talk later, Mistress Sarah,' he told her, and again she nodded as she left the room, after assuring herself that all was in order. She would have to talk to Robin Drummond. There was no escaping that interview. She could only hope that he would understand her reluctance and would, perhaps, wish to make his own arrangements, though being Master of Larraig, even for a few years, might be attractive to him.

Sir Thomas owned other properties as did Balwhidden, and he would not be ungenerous with his son-in-law. Together, with some of those lands bequeathed by Balwhidden, Robin might not fare badly.

But what sort of husband would he make? Sarah's lip curled when she compared him, as always, with the handsome Douglas. Robbie was a poor figure of a man compared with that nobleman.

* * *

Robin Drummond slept a round of the clock, then rose much refreshed and, after washing fastidiously in water pulled from the well in the courtyard, and changing into his grey linen shirt and green velvet jerkin, he was ready to eat his dinner with the family in the Great Hall.

At her father's instigation, Sarah, too, had changed her gown for one of pale blue velvet, but she had scorned the starched headdress which Anna Hyslop would have her wear and instead combed out her long golden curls and secured them beneath a small velvet cap seeded with pearls. Her black eyes, sparkling as brightly as Robin's, were like black diamonds as he appraised her from top to toe.

'You have blossomed into great beauty, Mistress Sarah,' he said, gallantly. 'Truly I am a fortunate man.'

He bowed and she caught a look of mischief in his own bright blue eyes, and her cheeks flamed. Sometimes she sensed that he was laughing at her, and she was in no mood to be the butt of his jokes.

'I do not know why you should consider yourself fortunate because of ... of my looks,' she returned.

Again he grinned with amusement. 'Do you not then? Yet I understand that your father has made it abundantly clear. After we have supped I would like an opportunity to discuss certain private matters with you, Mistress Sarah, if you would be so good as to arrange it.'

His skin was bronzed with exposure to the open air, but now that he had washed himself clean of dust and sweat, she could see that he was as fair-skinned as any girl. His hair was soft and fell over his forehead in black curls, but although he was not very tall, he somehow gave the impression of being taller than she had imagined. And his chin was well-formed, but cleft in the middle.

Sarah sighed deeply. If she could not have Lord Douglas ... and deep within herself she knew that he only belonged in her dreams ... then she hoped to be matched with a strong brave man who would take the responsibility for their lives on to his own shoulders. Since her mother died, and her grandmother had become weakened, she had been required to shoulder some of the responsibility for Larraig, and secretly she had sometimes grown tired of listening to the complaints of tenants and farmers living on the estate. Although she would never admit it to her father, she had longed at times for freedom from such responsibility, but if she married Robin Drummond, she would surely end up the man of the partnership, and be the one to give instructions and manage their affairs, instead of relying on the strength of a good husband. Her father must be mad not to recognize this. The dunt on his head had addled his brains, Sarah decided, because he had never before favoured Robbie Drummond.

At least he was not too fussy over his food. They had sometimes entertained foreign travellers journeying from Edinburgh to the west and Sir Thomas had been incensed by their pernickety manners, although he had also remembered the manners of a good host, and had not taken them to task.

Now their fare was poorer than it might have been since their best meat had gone with the men who rode beside Sir Thomas when they went to join the King. The lesser meat had gone to those left at Larraig, but the cooks were spicing it well with some of the new spices which the King had encouraged amongst the imports, and the food was tolerably well-cooked, even if strange to the taste.

Robin enjoyed every dish and complimented the cook so that John Dykes softened towards him and found him a honey pudding much to his liking.

After supper Lady Margaret went to her

chamber, helped by one of the maidservants. The weather had become wet and chilly and her bones ached in every joint as she climbed the stone stairs. She had been informed that Sir Thomas had negotiated a match between young Drummond and Sarah, and although she thought that perhaps Thomas could have done better for his daughter, she agreed that it was time the girl had a husband.

Nevertheless she rose reluctantly to leave the Great Hall unsure that the coming interview would be in the best interests of her granddaughter. But she and Drummond had to talk and make plans for their future, though the unsettled state of the country seemed to reflect the unsettled state of Larraig. Nothing appeared real or stable as it had been before King James gathered his army about him for battle. It was a stupid war, thought Lady Margaret, and had lost them their powerful King and left a babe in his place. The kingdom was unsettled and when that happened, wrong decisions were sometimes made. She had seen it happen before.

Robin Drummond politely escorted the Lady of Larraig, leaning heavily on the arm of a maidservant, from the Great Hall, then he came back to sit beside Sarah in front of the glowing embers of a huge log fire, augmented with sea coal. His manners were as polished as the most fastidious of Englishmen, and sometimes Sarah found this very pleasant. He took trouble to attend to the comforts of others. She had encountered many nobles when she served at Court, and although they did their best with the gallantries under the eyes of Queen Margaret, few accomplished elegance and grace like Robin Drummond. It was surely an affectation, she thought.

'It is fitting that we talk alone, Mistress Sarah,' he said when he had assured himself that she was comfortable, 'And glad I am to do so. I understand that Sir Thomas has spoken to you about a match between us. I hope that match is to your liking?'

His eyes shone with blue light reflected by the glowing embers of the fire and she moved uncomfortably as she sought to avoid staring into that bright gaze. She scarcely knew what to say. Should she pretend that she was happy to do her father's bidding, or should she be truthful and tell him it was abhorrent to her, and that she had no love for him?

She was not good at pretending, and his close scrutiny brought the defiant colour to her cheeks.

'I can see it is *not* to your liking, Mistress Sarah,' he said, softly. 'Well, it may not be to my liking either to wed a young woman who does not appreciate my worth as a husband. It may be that I am far from pleased with the arrangement. I have travelled in France and in England, Miss Sarah, and I have been entertained by ladies whose beauty beggars description, so that it disappoints me that I must take to my bed a raw young woman who is a beauty when she tries, but is often very careless of her appearance and has not the courtesy to wear a clean over-dress and bonnet when she dines with me.'

Sarah's cheeks were now flaming with colour and her eyes sparkled in her anger. Her gown might not be scrupulously clean, but it was one of her finest Court gowns.

'How dare you come here to insult me, Robin Drummond?' she asked, 'and while you have the hospitality of Larraig to welcome you. You primp and mince with supposedly good manners, but they are not *my* code, sir.'

'Do you have a code, Mistress?' he asked, silkily. 'It appears to me that Sir Thomas has allowed you to be reared by the servants. Look at your hair! How much time do you spend on its tangles? You do not even wear a fashionable head-dress yet the ladies of my country are as well-gowned as any when they try.'

'You boast of your elegant ladies,' she cried, furiously, 'but how many of them see you as a man, and not a pretty boy? You are an expert on the pretty behaviour of ladies, Robin Drummond, because you are not far from being one yourself!'

She saw his eyes change from devilment and amusement to the hardness of real anger.

'Is *that* what you think?' he asked in a very quiet voice. 'Well, I shall neither confirm nor deny anything to *you*, Mistress, but if you think a pretty boy cannot kiss a woman like a man, then you have much to learn.'

Suddenly she was pulled towards him and his slender elegant arms closed like iron traps about her body. His mouth was cool and hard on her own as he kissed her, but again the kisses were so demanding that her soft mouth felt bruised before he let her go. His skin had been soft and smooth next to her own, and the strength of his lips had stirred her strangely.

'You are like an animal!' she cried, hardly knowing what she was saying, 'the kind of animal which is smooth and ... sleek outside yet is ferocious for all that.'

'Not quite such a pretty boy?' he asked, silkily.

'Only because you wish to ... to humiliate me,' she cried. 'You can be what you like, when you like, when you want to deny me my words.'

'Then if you doubt my motives, how can we talk together?' he asked, rather wearily. 'The truth is that Sir Thomas has negotiated the match with my own father, and we must each of us put our own feelings in check and accept the arrangement. It is best for Larraig and for Balwhidden, though I had other plans for my own life, as you apparently had for yours. We have fought each other in the past and have depleted the estates in anger and strife. Now it is time for us to stand together and a match between us makes good sense. Try to accept it with that same good sense.'

She stared at him angrily. 'I am merely a pawn in the kind of chess game my father taught me to play.'

'Games can be won by the judicious use of a pawn,' he returned, and anger again struck blindly at her heart. This man was cold and hard inside. He appeared to be gentle as a woman but he was hard, as hard as the diamonds worn by the Queen, as the sapphires which matched his eyes.

'My father lies wounded,' she said, 'as does your brother at Balwhidden, and most of our noblemen who escaped death on the field, but you, sir, have not a mark on your person. You appear to be well versed in avoiding weapons wielded by our enemies.'

He went very pale. 'But not so good at avoiding the weapons of the woman I have been ordered to wed ... your tongue, Madam. You wish for honesty. Well, I will be honest. I do not like the match any more than you do. I have worries enough without taking on the responsibility of a spoilt, pert, ignorant child who must surely have been well-versed in avoiding the spankings she so richly deserved when growing up. Aye, even then I saw you for what you were, a lass who would grow up to be useless for anything other than breeding sons who might grow up, given a good strong father, to be better than their mother!'

'Now I am a brood mare!'

'Take good care if I renege, even though I love the bravery and gallantry of your father, and respect my own. I take you for *their* sakes, not yours!'

'You will *never* take me!' she cried furiously. 'Whether you like it or not, I am a woman in my own right, and women are no longer so subservient to men. Women have to keep the castle whilst the men go out and kill one another...'

'Yet I disappoint you because I knew how to avoid the blows of my enemies,' he interrupted. 'I should have bared my breast to them and invited a dirty English sword or bill to cut me to ribbons so that a foolish young woman might admire my bravery. You cannot blame a man for fighting his enemies, then blame him yet again for not fighting.'

'Oh... you! You twist my words. You try to make me look foolish!'

'Not very difficult, Mistress Sarah. You *are* foolish, but you have the makings of a fine woman in you. That is how I reassured myself when the proposition was put to me.'

'How can you say such things to me?' Sarah asked, too angry to speak above a whisper.

There were a great many younger sons who would be very happy to make a match with the daughter of Larraig, yet here was Robin Drummond telling her what a sacrifice he must make by accepting her in marriage!

'You are the *last* man I would choose for myself,' she said, holding her head very high. 'I will see my father and ... and plead with him to reconsider. I will go on my bended knees, if necessary.'

'Make a good petition then,' Robin told her, cheerfully. 'It will be to my benefit as well as your own.'

Sarah rose to her feet with great dignity.

'I will retire now, sir. We have nothing more to say to one another. Good-night.'

'If your father will not be moved, then we wed within two weeks,' he told her. 'The priest has already been informed and you will be obliged to stand up with me then.'

She gasped. 'It is too soon!'

'Aye, that I agree, but Sir Thomas was set on it and made the arrangements. There is much to be done at Larraig and he thinks I will have more authority to order the estate if I am his son-in-law.'

Sarah forgot that she had ever wanted to be free of responsibility.

'I can take care of anything which requires to be done,' she cried.

'For how long? The lazy rascals who serve you soon know when the master's voice is weakened, and pay little heed to a woman of your years. They would pay more attention to Lady Margaret, who is old and feeble and should have quiet peaceful days to enjoy her rest. They need the whip cracked over their heads, or over their backs if their laziness persists, or the well will be poisoned with filth.'

'You would rather clean the castle than fortify it against our enemies.'

'Dirt and filth and squalor *are* my enemies,' he told her. 'Now, Mistress Sarah, I will escort you to your bedchamber, then retire to my own. You are fortunate that I am not a ruffian or I might prefer to remain with you till morn, though perhaps that is how *you* would prefer to be treated. Pick up your bonnet. It has fallen from your head.'

'I can attend to myself, sir and John Dykes will attend to the fire if it has burned low. I can escort myself to my own bedchamber.'

'Where is your maidservant?'

'I have none to attend me about my person. You condemn me for working like one of my own servants, but I can think of no better way for a woman with my responsibilities to grow up, sir. I refuse to be your idle, languishing lady, sir, so be warned. If your greed for power, the power which would come to you as son-in-law to Larraig, overcomes your distaste for taking an ignorant peasant girl like myself to wife, I hereby give notice that I shall remain so all my life.'

Again his eyes were gleaming and his lips quirked as though with hidden laughter as he regarded her very steadily.

'Then I will say goodnight here, Mistress.'

Before she divined his intentions, he pulled

her into his arms and kissed her deliberately on the lips. This time his mouth was cool and sweet on her own.

Pulling away she hurried towards the stone stairs which led to the bedchambers on the upper floor. Her own led directly out of her grandmother's room, and she crept quietly through the chamber trying to avoid disturbing the older lady. But Lady Margaret was still wakeful.

'Have you fixed up the date of the ceremony?' she asked.

Sarah paused, then came over to the large bed and looked at the old lady.

'I am not happy with the match, Grandmother,' she said, a sob beginning to rise in her throat.

'Have you heard the list of men who will never return from Flodden?' the old lady asked. 'Those who are left can pick and choose, the finest flowers of the field.'

'I know that is true,' Sarah said, bitterly. 'Robin Drummond was not slow to remind me.'

'Devil take him,' Lady Margaret muttered. 'That is a fine way for a gentleman to woo a lady when he would make her his bride!'

'He ... he thinks I am no better than a servant, either in looks or manners. He has spent some time telling me so. He is used to associating with a great many more elegant ladies.'

Lady Margaret heaved herself further up in bed and raised her eyebrows.

'Do you tell me so? Devil take him!' she repeated. 'He is an impertinent rogue. Thomas has allowed that young fellow to get above himself. He clings to him as though he were already his son.' She stared at Sarah. 'You do not think, then, that he will win your heart in time?'

'I am certain he will not!' Tears of anger and humiliation shone in her eyes, and Lady Margaret again lay back to consider the matter.

'Go to bed, child,' she said at length. 'We will see what Master Drummond has to say for himself in the morning.'

CHAPTER SEVEN

Sir Thomas felt well enough to demand that he should be allowed out of bed, and no one else but Robin, aided by John Dykes, was allowed to help him. Anna Hyslop, who scolded him unmercifully, was banished from the room. His 'longshanks' were his own affair and not to be twittered over by his womenfolk.

Even so, Sarah was shocked by his frail appearance when he was finally brought to sit by the huge log fire in the Great Hall, though a warning look on Robin Drummond's face bade her be silent.

Lady Margaret took a long look, then raised her eyes to the ceiling.

'By Heaven, Thomas, but you have lost your flesh,' she said, loudly. 'I will supervise your meat to the last portion. You have been feeding the dogs with it whilst in bed, just as I suspected, and now they rove around you like wolves.'

Sir Thomas looked sheepish.

'A bit now and then is no hurt to the creatures who serve us well, but it is true that I must gain my strength to celebrate my daughter's wedding to young Robbie, here. Give me the two weeks to get back my strength then we will be at the revelry. That will give the sewing woman time to stitch your gown, Sarah, and you can go to Edinburgh and buy the best of the silks and velvets with all fancy embroidery to delight your heart. My daughter will not go to her wedding in a shabby gown, that I promise.'

Sarah's cheeks coloured rosily and she darted a venomous look at Robin, but his eyes were engaged elsewhere. How could they expect her to have joy in preparing a wedding gown when she was so ill-matched to her bridegroom?

This morning he wore wine velvet embroidered with silver and his blue eyes were clear and guileless as those of a child. Yet they could harden into blue ice, as she well knew, so that she could almost feel afraid of him.

'I have heard news that the booths in Edinburgh are growing empty already since the battle was lost,' she said. 'Every traveller says that is true.'

'A ploy to make you buy their wares,' her father returned. 'It will be gossip for the packmen, I have no doubt.'

'We have silks a-plenty. The gown can be made at Larraig,' Lady Margaret said in a voice which brooked no argument. 'The gown is but the trappings. The wedding is good or ill according to the pleasures of the couple to be wed. And a fine gown will not make a fine lady.' She glared at Robin. 'Have ye considered that, Thomas?'

Again Sarah was well aware that Robin was listening intently though he made no sign that he had heard.

'Everything has been agreed with Balwhidden,' Sir Thomas said angrily. 'I will not have it otherwise, and enough of such talk. It takes my strength away to argue with womenfolk.'

Sarah saw that her father looked white and strained and her heart faltered. She could do little else other than go along with his wishes, though she was certain that Robin Drummond had no more taste for her than she had for him.

Suddenly she had sympathy for him. He was being forced into the match as well as herself, and he would be forced to live at Larraig though it was not his home or ever likely to be. He would have preferred to marry a fine lady, well-powdered and scented. There were plenty of that sort at Court, and some of them glad of a husband like Robin. She had had no time to ape them, busy as she was with helping Lady Jane Hamilton to nurse Prince Jamie ... now King James V ... and Lady Jane was a plain woman with no pandering to fashion whatsoever.

The baby King James had now been crowned at Stirling and her father would have been bidden to attend had he not been ill of his wounds, but Robin had been there and would tell her nothing, other than the fact that the Douglases and the Hamiltons were jostling for position in caring for the child and influencing the Queen Regent.

'Like dogs fighting over a bone,' Robin told her, grimly. 'It is a pity the poor babe cannot be rent in two.'

'Do not say so, even in jest,' she returned. 'I have helped nurse the child, and he is like my own son to me. He will be a great king one day.'

'Aye, and a lot of days have to be lived through until he is fit to hold the crown of Scotland on his head, and to keep the great barons in their place.'

Sarah sighed and tried to accept that her life of carefree happiness was over before it had ever begun. There was no escape from this marriage to Robin Drummond. Her father was weakened and Robin was correct when he said that a strong hand was needed to keep the rascally tenants up to their tasks, in order that the estate was well run and productive.

Food was needed more than ever in the aftermath of such a battle as had never been fought in their history. The total number of good men who had perished on the battlefield was now assessed at ten thousand, with five thousand lost to the English. And the loss was even more serious for Scotland if one considered the rank and quality of those slain. The English lost few men of rank and distinction, but the Scots had lost earls, bishops, lords and sons of peers, and few families had not lost at least one relative or close friend. When the full extent of their losses had been received at Larraig, Sir Thomas and Robin Drummond had been greatly saddened by the figures, and Sarah had gone about her duties without further argument. It was a sad time for their country.

Robin took over Sarah's duties in running the estate after the announcement had been made that they were betrothed and he would be son-in-law to Sir Thomas within fourteen days.

At first there were those who would have treated him with scant respect, as they had been doing with Sarah, but after an argument with one great burly fellow, Robin Drummond had picked him up and hurled him to the ground, knocking the wind clean out of the man. Word had got around that he had magic powers in his slender body and soon the neglect at Larraig was being put to rights and repairs to property carried out before the worst of the winter weather came upon them.

Lady Margaret had been busy sending out notes of invitation and a week before the wedding a special messenger arrived so that Sarah did not at first realize that the messenger was from Court. When she did, her cheeks flushed and her eyes sparkled with excitement. The message was from Lady Jame Hamilton and informed her that the Queen Regent wished to engage her services once again in the care of King James V. Now that Jamie was King, there was a good deal more to be done in caring for him and Lady Jane needed good, competent help such as Sarah would be able to give. The Queen Regent needed all her friends about her and if Mistress Sarah could come, even for a few weeks, it would be helpful to Lady Jane.

Sir Thomas considered the matter carefully whilst Sarah waited with her nerves strung to breaking point. Was this the open door for which she had prayed? Would she see Douglas again? Would he be at Court? At one time she would have clamoured to be allowed to leave immediately, but she was learning how to grow up very fast, and waited quietly for her father's decision.

'You have been bidden to serve the Queen

Regent,' he said at last, having studied the message, 'and I have no power to deny you that privilege.'

'Oh Father!' she cried with delight.

'We will hurry on the wedding,' he ended and her spirits tumbled immediately. She turned to look at Robin Drummond with her dismay clearly written on her face, and after a long moment he smiled in return.

'Why not?' he asked, maliciously. 'The priest can perform the ceremony tomorrow. We can be wed before you go, Mistress Sarah, so that you need not be disappointed and be required to postpone your wedding day.'

She ran her tongue over her dry lips. 'My gown is not yet ready,' she protested.

'I never thought to hear you voicing concern over your clothes. As I understand it, a fine gown does not make a fine bride. I am sure the one you are wearing will suit you charmingly,' Robin told her, bowing.

Sarah coloured furiously. She wore an old gown which was too small for her and which she had covered with an apron. She had been helping to remove smoke grime from the hangings in the Great Hall in preparation for guests arriving for the wedding.

'We can leave the matter of a wedding until Mistress Sarah returns from Court,' Robin said at length. 'I would not want to hurry it along. We have no babe to be born illegitimately. Do not distress her further, Sir Thomas.'

Again she felt the warm colour rushing back into her cheeks and she dropped her eyes. Robin could accuse her of lack of manners, but he was very forthright when he, himself, chose. Such remarks brought home to her how personal their relationship would be.

'I need you beside me, Robbie, as a son. Jamie is too young, and I am not fit to keep the place. Let Sarah go to Court, if the Queen demands it, but she must go as your wife.'

'Do not forget that we are now betrothed. Mistress Sarah is wearing my betrothal ring and that is sufficient until a wedding to please her can be arranged.'

'She is better to be wearing your wedding ring,' Sir Thomas growled. 'See to it.'

'But I am bidden *now*, Father.'

'You can travel when you are ready. The messenger will require to rest. We can celebrate as we can and have a fine banquet when you have returned from Court, Sarah. The Queen Regent cannot keep you by her side for too long if you have a husband waiting for your return and it is not my wish that you should serve at Court for a long time. Lady Jane Hamilton is old and some of the Court ladies are not in the marriage market, or are widowed.'

Lady Margaret sighed deeply. She was listening avidly and now she decided that she had done her best, and could do no more.

Perhaps Thomas had the right of it. Perhaps it would be better if Sarah were wed and Robin Drummond was not such a bad match as she had feared. She had been talking more to the boy and thought that Thomas was not such a fool after all.

The gown, too, could be finished with less beads and embroidery, and the kitchen had been busy for several days preparing pies and sweetmeats. It could be done.

She looked at her granddaughter and sighed again. It was hard for a woman ... aye, but hard, too, to be a man. One could only trust in God that all would be well.

'Go to your room, child,' she told Sarah, kindly. 'Today is your wedding day. I will see that all is done properly for you, and we will call in our friends from nearby to see the knot tied. There will be time for that if we summon them now.'

Sarah's eyes met those of Robin Drummond but his face was without expression. Had he, too, hoped for a miracle so that he need not go through with this bargain? She could not guess how he felt, but at least she would be able to stay in Court for some weeks until she had come to terms with what Fate held in store for her. Maybe ... maybe she would see Douglas again. Maybe her life would not seem so bleak if she could see him just once more.

But there was no escape from this wedding.

Slowly she turned away and made for the

dark stone stairs. They were as cold and bleak as her own heart.

* * *

Sarah scarcely knew how her grandmother accomplished it, but news of the new wedding date spread fast, and in no time people were riding in and the traditional feast with sports and musical entertainment was being arranged so that by the time she was groomed and ready, a fair-sized crowd had gathered to see her married.

The Drummonds of Balwhidden had gathered in force being their nearest neighbour as well as the bridegroom's family, and even Archibald, Robin's elder brother, still sick of his wounds, had been carried to Larraig and loudly mourned his injuries which had delayed his own wedding and which now prevented him from dancing with his new sister, or jousting, or wrestling.

'I should have looked to you myself, Sister Sarah,' he told her, shaking his head, 'had not my brother first warmed to your beauty. My wound is a scourge. Like many an old quarrel, it heals on top but not underneath.'

'I will see what my grandmother can do for you, Archibald,' she promised.

'I have enough auld wives round me to have me reborn into the next world,' he said, wearily. 'Let the surgeon do his worst. He is a good fellow.'

Sarah said no more. Word had come that her gown was ready, and the seamstress with two maids helped her to dress. It was of gossamer silk, sewn with pearls and richly embroidered with silver thread. She wore a tall headdress, also sewn with pearls on her long shining silvery hair. She had been scrubbed clean by Anna Hyslop who advocated that she must now live the life of a lady and bath regularly in scented water. Then she had been helped by two more serving-maids into the beautiful silk gown, the neckline trimmed with lace so gossamer fine that it had taken the lacemakers many hours to fashion more than an inch.

When they were gowned, Lady Margaret, clad in pale grey velvet with a white silk headdress and many jewelled rings on her slender fingers now knobbled with rheumatism, came to look at her critically. Her black eyes, so like Sarah's, misted with tears as she recognized that her granddaughter had grown into a beautiful woman. Thomas had been right to hurry on the wedding before Sarah left for Court. There was many a rascal hanging round the Queen's skirts with nothing better to do than pay Court to the more beautiful amongst her ladies.

But would she be happy with Drummond? Lady Margaret sighed again. He was certainly different as a man from the one who had wedded her many years ago, but Thomas set store by him. At first she had thought that Thomas's judgement was faulty because of his weakened state, and because it was young Robbie who had carried him home from Flodden, but Thomas had dismissed these fancies with a wave of his hand.

'I know the lad better than you, Mother,' he said firmly. 'There is nothing wrong with young Robbie that time and a good wife will not cure. Take more time to talk to the lad, Mother.'

She had done so and was now concerned for him as well as for Sarah. What sort of wife would she make if she did not love him? She had been allowed her own way for too long. She was a strong-willed girl and now she was a beautiful young woman, and Robin knew it whatever he said.

Ah well, she would put her worries into God's hands through her daily worship. There was little more that an old woman of her years could do.

* * *

The groom almost outshone the bride for the magnificence of his attire, and one of Sarah's maids said she had heard it from Robin Drummond's manservant that he had bought his clothes in France.

'Nor would he have been the peacock there, Mistress Sarah, because all nobles dress in silks and satins in France. Master Drummond had the suit made so that he would look as fine as any at Court, and now his servant says he will wear it for the wedding.'

'I do not care what he wears,' said Sarah, snappishly, then regretted the words when she saw the veiled looks which her words provoked. It would cast a shadow over everything if it was known that the bride was not willing.

She turned again to smile at the young maid. 'I am full of nerves and fears,' she said. 'My bridal gown feels strange to me.'

Both maidservants laughed and assured her that it was perfect for a bride and would be talked about in Larraig for many a day.

Robin's appearance had not been exaggerated and Sarah's eyes widened when she saw that he was dressed in gold and silver brocaded satin, with lace at his throat and wrists. He looked elegant and dandified compared with the majority of their guests.

His blue eyes sparkled brightly as they travelled over her slowly from head to foot.

'It is as I thought,' he murmured. 'You look charming, Mistress Sarah. We would neither of us disgrace the Court of France.'

'The Court of Scotland will do very well for me, sir,' she returned and again his eyes gleamed.

'I have not forgotten that I am about to lose my new bride ... tomorrow.'

The last word was spoken very softly and her heart missed a beat, then raced almost uncontrollably. She had thought that she would ride out of Larraig for Stirling as soon as the wedding was celebrated, but now Robin was reminding her that she would leave her home as a wife, and not merely a bride.

'Come, Sarah, I think all is ready for us,' he told her, briskly, and together they faced the priest who wedded them with an ease out of all proportion to the magnitude of such a ceremony.

Then the celebrations began and as dusk fell, the courtyard was lighted as more and more guests arrived and the games and revelry grew more and more noisy as wine and ale flowed freely, and the food was eaten with noisy enjoyment. Only the dogs were quieter as they lay sleeping in corners, worn out with excited barking and feasting on plentiful scraps of food.

The kitchens had been augmented from Balwhidden as their party arrived, and Robin's father and mother were well entertained by Sir Thomas and Lady Margaret. It was the first joyous occasion in the neighbourhood since the grim results of Flodden had gradually crept up from the south, and it seemed to Sarah that there was almost a feverish quality about the proceedings.

Robin was invited to take part in the wrestling bouts but he smilingly shook his head, even though Sir Thomas offered to hold his fine coat for him.

Sarah, remembering that he had settled a swaggering servant's impertinence by throwing the fellow to the ground, encouraged him to participate like any bridegroom. They had already danced a reel or two after the feast had been cleared away from the Great Hall and passed on to the poorer people and the children who swarmed around hungrily. But Robin refused to put his skill to the test.

'Why not?' Sarah demanded, as she turned to him hopefully. She would dearly have loved to feel proud of his prowess, but instead he was showing himself craven in front of all their guests.

'Because I would rather drink this excellent wine,' he told her, a trifle thickly, and she began to suspect that Robin was becoming drunk like some of the other men. She wanted to protest but something stayed her tongue. If he were drunk, then he would be thrown into their marriage bed and allowed to snore until morning. He would not be the first bridegroom to be oblivious of his own wedding night.

'Drink it then,' she encouraged, harshly. 'Drink it to the last drop.'

* * *

The noise was still at its height when Sarah's maidservants came to find her and to conduct her to the bridal chamber prepared for her and Robin. His mother, Lady Elspeth Drummond, came to take her hand then kiss her cheek.

'You are a Drummond now,' she said, 'and I am sure you will be as proud of Balwhidden as you have been of Larraig.'

'I will try to uphold the honour of both families,' she said, steadily. 'I hope that my ... my husband feels the same desire.'

'There is no man more conscious of his duties than your new husband, Mistress Drummond,' Lady Elspeth said with dignity. 'He may wear fine feathers, but he is also a very fine bird.'

'He leads out my grandmother in a dance,' said Sarah, watching the stately progress of one of their more sedate dances.

'She has a young heart,' Lady Elspeth said as she watched, 'and is a very fine lady. There was a time when we were not always the best of friends, but Lady Margaret Graham could always talk sense into the men. We are more prosperous now that we do not have to feed a great many men around us, ready to rush out and fight one another, though this last battle has taken much in the way of reserves, and has cost us many lives which we mourn every day. But now we must build again, and I feel that Robin's marriage to you, my dear Sarah, makes a new beginning. You and he can build together.'

Sarah was saved from replying by the arrival

of her ladies and her maidservants, bent on disrobing her and putting on the finest of cotton gowns well trimmed with lace, for her marriage bed.

She looked for Robin. He was singing loudly and quite musically, and Lady Margaret was joining in with a surprisingly strong contralto. It was a song which made some of the ladies blush and giggle, and Sarah was sure that Robin was now well into his cups. The revelry would last for many hours yet, so she allowed herself to be led away.

CHAPTER EIGHT

The excitement of the wedding had chased all thoughts of sleep from Sarah's head and she felt strange and unreal in her fresh nightgown and sheets which were cold despite the warming bricks.

In the courtyard the revelry continued as though it were an almost feverish reaction from the quiet days of foreboding when the men were riding south to stand beside the King. The country had grown sick, but now and again there could be moments of joy, as was usual in life. A shaft of sunlight could sometimes pierce the darkest clouds, thought Sarah, though her own clouds blotted out all sunshine until she returned to Court, then the sun might shine from the eyes of Douglas. He was safe and well, she remembered, and her heart warmed.

The noise began to lull Sarah's senses even as her nerves had been soothed with a goblet of wine. Drummond would not come tonight. His men would carry him off to further revelry and he would sleep off his wine in the nearest corner. Some lusty farmer's daughter might even cradle him in her arms, thought Sarah, with curling lip. He might not be obliged to prove his new manhood with her. Her eyelids drooped and she slept.

Suddenly she was jerked awake as a silent figure walked into the chamber and began to unbuckle his clothing. He stirred the log fire, a rare concession to comfort, with his toe and the leaping flames reflected the slender figure of Robin Drummond, grotesquely elongated, as it was thrown on to the ceiling.

'What are *you* doing here?' she demanded, stupidly. 'I ... I beg pardon ... but why have you come?'

He had stripped out of his clothing and now he came to grin at her, almost fiendishly, as she lay on the large bed.

'Why do you think I have come to my own bed? I have come to claim my bride. Why should you be surprised by that, Mistress Drummond? It would surely be very strange if I did not come.'

Her eyes widened and she shrank against the pillows.

'But... but you were drunk!' she cried. 'You were in your cups.'

'Was I? Am I? Why should I drink myself senseless on my wedding night when I am abstemious in my habits at all other times? I do not like to have my mind addled with wine. It served me ill in the past and made me vulnerable when I should have kept a clear head. A man must learn these things when he is still little more than a boy.'

He leapt into bed beside her and pulled her now-warm body towards his own.

'God, but the bed is a cold one,' he told her. 'You will have to warm my heart, my dear wife.'

'Will anything warm your heart?' she demanded.

'You will have no cause for complaint, that I promise you. Have I not played my part in providing you with a good wedding, one which you will remember until we are both old and grey.'

'You preferred wine to wrestling,' she reminded him. 'I think you *are* drunk!'

'Then why have me wrestle with some poor fool?'

'You were afraid he would throw you to the floor, yet I have seen you throw a man with larger build than yourself.'

He sighed deeply and began to play with her hair.

'Such pretty hair when it is clean and shining. It gleams like silver in the firelight. Ah yes, that rascal who needed a lesson. I had to teach that one his manners. When I was in France, I mis-spent my early years and drank too deeply at times of their wine, and...'

'Loved their women?'

'Perhaps. They were charming to me. But one evening I went to the wrong establishment and did not know then that I should not drink wine enough to leave my body vulnerable to thieves, robbers and worse. I was set upon as I left the gaming-house, and had it not been for a gentleman, even more slender than myself, intervening on my behalf, you would not be the bride of Robin Drummond this night.'

'Oh?' Despite herself Sarah was interested. 'What did he do, Robin?'

'He threw my assailants against a wall and one of them broke his neck.'

'How... how dreadful,' she said, shivering. She was used to sword-play and could handle a weapon herself, but to have one's neck snapped seemed a horrifying prospect.

'We became friends,' said Robin, still pulling gently at her curls. 'He taught me how to use my body so that a large man's weight and strength could be used against himself. But he made me promise to use the skill in a circumspect fashion. If a rascal needs a lesson, why then I teach it, but I do not throw a man to the floor in order to entertain others. Can you understand that, Sarah?'

She could not make any reply because suddenly his warm firm lips claimed her own and she was held, powerless, in a pair of sinewy arms.

'You do not have scruples when you demonstrate your skills to me,' Sarah gasped as she managed to push him away. She could see his white even teeth as he grinned at her in the firelight.

'I have even greater skills to show you,' he told her. 'Now, do not fight me and you will not get hurt. You know we must consummate our marriage and there is no time to woo you gently before deflowering you. When you return to Court, you go as my wife, and when you return *from* Court, I shall woo you properly, but for now I do not intend to shilly-shally about making you my wife.'

'I will not have you touch me!' Sarah hissed, her heart now bounding with fright. She had thought Robin Drummond a soft man, but there was nothing soft about the taut well-muscled body which was claiming her own.

'You have no choice, my white heart,' he said. 'We are one under God and the Law.'

She cried out, then turned her head into the pillow and presently he cradled her once again in his arms.

'There. It was not such an ordeal, was it? Soon you will not be fighting me. We must pass on the gift of life to a new generation and that is the purpose of the ceremony the priest performed, and of the negotiations between our families.'

'But you do not love me,' she said, tears beginning to trickle from her eyes. This man was now her husband, and had taken everything which had belonged to herself, alone.

'You mean that *you* do not love *me*,' he said in a colourless voice. 'You have left me in no doubt about that and therefore you do not make yourself attractive to me. You languished after Douglas, did you not? Well, he is the Earl of Angus now and head of his house. He raises his sights high though he is not good enough for Sarah Graham. He is not fit to be your husband.'

'And you are?'

The tears were coming faster, but he had goaded her into making the remark. How did he know she loved Douglas? Had it been so obvious to anyone who cared to look at her?

'Certainly,' he was saying. 'I am the only man who is suitable for you.'

'Yet you think yourself too good for me, also, and ... and you have hurt me.'

He muttered something under his breath and pulled her into his arms again.

'You will feel better soon. Do not be such a babe. It will be better next time.'

'Next time!'

'But of course! I do not admire your

innocence, Sarah. I wonder how Angus would have treated you, though if he laid a finger on you, I would be obliged to use every violent skill at my command on him, and that would not be wise.'

Sarah shivered again at the sudden menace in his tone.

'Why is he now the Earl of Angus?' she asked huskily. 'Surely his father...'

'Killed at Flodden Field, also his uncle. His grandfather, old Archibald Bell-the-Cat has not survived them for very long, so there is a new Earl of Angus posturing at Court. I give you fair warning that you go to Stirling as my wife. I shall look after Larraig, together with Lady Margaret and Sir Thomas and I will keep young Jamie under firm control until you return. After that we will have our own establishment within easy reach of Larraig and Balwhidden. We will found our own family and will be beholden to no man save the King whom we serve faithfully. You are a Drummond now, Sarah, so make the best of it. Get some sleep whilst there is still darkness.'

He turned over after kissing her again and she lay still beside him, still and stiff as a board. She was unused to sharing her bed except with her grandmother or Anna Hyslop when the thunder frightened her in childhood. Now she had been forced to intimate pursuits with Robin Drummond, and now she was a wife and not a maid.

And Douglas was so far above her that he would never be hers, even if she could be free of her marriage ties. And Drummond had ensured that their wedding vows were well witnessed and that he had taken possession of her. She was well and truly his.

Fatigue overcame her and she slept, and when Anna Hyslop came to jerk her out of her sleep, she found that she was alone in the marriage bed.

'Master Drummond is in the courtyard, attending to your escort, Mistress Sarah,' Anna told her. 'You are to ride well protected.'

Wearily Sarah crept out of bed.

* * *

Robin Drummond had decided he would escort his wife to Stirling. Since she was now a Drummond, his first duty was to her and not to Larraig, even though he had sworn to act as a true son to Sir Thomas and care for the place as though it were his own property.

Jamie would soon be old enough to go to school since the law demanded that the sons of all nobles were sent to school and taught their Latin in order that they could read the best books and documents. He was already learning these languages with the monks, but he needed to be attending classes with boys of his own age. Later he would study Law at St Andrews University, or perhaps Glasgow, which would help him to understand the running of Larraig and how the country was governed. Sir Thomas was interested in education and had supported King James in all his efforts to improve the educational system of the country.

He had taken pleasure in the books printed by Androw Myllar and Walter Chapman, and Robbie's delight in these books had helped to forge the bond between the two men. Thomas had taught Sarah to read and write though what was the sense of that, Lady Margaret could not see. It should surely be left to the scholars and the scribes to do that, and King James had opened another university at Aberdeen so there were enough men with learning to do all that was necessary.

Robin supervised the packing of his wife's personal effects, but he thought that her gowns had room for improvement. He had often travelled to Flanders as an envoy and many Flemings had come to settle in Scotland and their skills were being used to improve the quality of life. Silks, satins and velvets were imported from Flanders and Robin decided that there should be a wider choice of such materials available to provide his wife with new gowns despite the aftermath of Flodden. She should be able to live more graciously and he would organize changes to be made at Larraig to add to its comfort before her return.

Robin was a younger son, but he had a head

for commerce and had quietly amassed a considerable fortune by dealing with rich merchants who were glad to buy some of the fine pearls found in Scottish rivers, even as they provided wine, gold and silver thread in addition to the beautiful cloths which King James had encouraged for the pleasure of his subjects.

Their King would be sadly missed, thought Robin as he assembled his men in the courtyard. A barrel of salted fish was being removed from storage, fish bought from Ayr and Aberdeen. The fishermen in the seaport towns had been encouraged to land good catches as this was part of the country's riches. Who would safeguard those riches now? Robin wondered as he stood in the courtyard at Larraig and looked at some of the neglect and disorder he would require to attend to as soon as possible.

Queen Margaret would not give strong enough government, and some of the nobles were already casting their eyes towards France where the Duke of Albany, cousin to King James, lived in exile.

Albany was closely allied to France, Robin remembered, and King Henry of England would not be happy if he came back to rule Scotland, not only because he would be ousting his sister, the Queen Regent, but because of that close link with France. And Henry had defeated their armies at Flodden and could well march into their country to press home his advantage.

Larraig was vulnerable, thought Robin, as was Balwhidden, should Surrey decide to march north. He would be wise to leave Sarah at Court to serve the Queen and return immediately.

*   *   *

Sarah hardly knew whether she was glad or sorry when Robin escorted her safely to Stirling Castle, then rounded his men in order to return immediately to Larraig. He had taken charge so efficiently that for a little while it had been very pleasant to allow herself to be cared for by this man who was now her husband.

In other circumstances, it might be pleasant to have such a husband, but she had not forgotten that marriage involved other duties less to her liking. She had not forgotten her wedding night and when Robin briskly bade her assemble her extra belongings where his men could pack them on the ponies, she had turned a reddened cheek away from him. He remained discreetly in the background when she bade farewell to her family, then Robin escorted her to the courtyard where she was well and comfortably mounted on a good horse. As the weeks had passed into months, the fear of Surrey had lessened and it seemed that King Henry of England would not press home his advantage, but it was expedient to take all care when making a journey.

'King Henry has respect for his sister's wishes,' Robin remarked as they rode side by side. 'She reminded him that she is now Queen Regent and Henry took heed. It was better so.'

Nevertheless the countryside looked more unkempt and deserted than usual. Men had been lost at Flodden who would have been better employed working the land and tending the flocks of sheep. The weakness of government was now laying its mark on the land, much to Robin's concern as he looked about him on all sides then urged his horse to ride beside Sarah towards Stirling.

'Boys will have to grow into men,' he told Sarah, 'and their sisters required to take their place.'

'As I was,' said Sarah, a trifle sharply, 'though it appears that you take my place, sir.'

'Larraig requires more than boys or girls to make it prosperous again. Some of the fields have not been ploughed for corn and the sheep are not shepherded so that they are wild on the hills. I will attend to Larraig, never fear, and your father and grandmother. It would have been no task for a woman of your years.'

She relaxed in the saddle. There was something strong about Robin which did not always show on the surface. She truly believed that no harm would come to her family or her home whilst he was in charge of them, and a faint feeling of regret lay on her heart that she was obliged to leave them and return to Court to serve the Queen Regent.

She sat up more stiffly in the saddle. What thoughts were these? She should be more than thankful to be spared a wife's more intimate duties for a few months longer. She stole a glance at Robin. His face was stronger than she had imagined, his chin firm and his mouth well controlled. She wondered how many women he had loved. Was there a special woman he had wanted who had been unattainable? A French lady, perhaps?

Sarah felt suddenly jealous of his past, then again pushed such thoughts behind her. She should not care about Drummond's past. Soon she might see Douglas, again, and even though she could only admire him from the shadows, it would be exciting to look upon his handsome upright figure once more.

An hour later they rode into Stirling.

CHAPTER NINE

The Court had moved to Edinburgh and Sarah had gone with all the other ladies, her own duties fairly onerous as assistant nursemaid to the newly crowned baby, King James V.

Lady Jane Hamilton had greeted her warmly, but Sarah was struck by the change in the older woman. Lady Jane appeared to have aged a great deal in the past few months and much of her brisk cheerful manner had deserted her. Instead she was subdued and her eyes darted about watchfully.

'The Court is swarming with Douglases,' she told Sarah, 'those who did not drop at Flodden. They seek to wrest the power away from all the other nobles. They would take charge of the King and I am suspect because I am a Hamilton. My own kinsman, Arran, who married our good King James's aunt ... sister to James the Third, as you know ... is thereby related to our royalty and so our family claim more rights than the Douglases. But they are going to set that to rights soon enough.'

'How?' asked Sarah as she began to sort through the clothes for the royal babe. He was a pale little boy, but bright and happy and she loved him even as she loved her own Jamie. A sudden curious sense of longing had assailed her when she lifted the child into her arms. It would be good to hold her own child one day. It would be good to be the mother of a fine son.

Although she pushed such thoughts away, they returned from time to time to disturb her, and she had strange longings which she did not fully comprehend. She was no longer the young girl who had been nursemaid to Prince Jamie before leaving Court to go home to Larraig all those weeks ago. She was now wife to Drummond.

'Angus has returned to Court,' Lady Jane said in a whisper. 'He dances attendance on the Queen.'

Sarah's heart bounded. Angus! So she would see him soon, this man who had occupied her dreams for so long. All thoughts of Robin Drummond and Larraig disappeared from her mind and she quickly searched for her prettiest gown before joining the other ladies for dinner. Lady Jane had insisted that Sarah should dine with the Court ladies in the Great Hall whilst she remained with the baby king. She had several young maidservants to help in the nursery, but she had been pleased to welcome Sarah back to Court and from a chance remark, the girl began to wonder if her grandmother had been responsible for this summons. She questioned Lady Jane, but the old woman merely shook her head.

' 'Tis best you be here,' she said. 'You are not a Douglas nor owe them any allegiance. You are not a Hamilton either, as I am, and you have experience in tending our wee man. He is our babe, even if he is the King, poor lad. It will be a long time before he holds his own crown on his head and the kingdom in his own hands.'

Changes were everywhere, thought Sarah, after they moved to Edinburgh which was now the capital city since King James had decreed it so. The wall against invasion had been built and there was an oppressive, uneasy cloud hanging over the whole city. Gone was the happiness and gaiety when people bought freely of fine silks, linen, jewels and exotic imported spices in the booths. It was like a city still mourning its dead.

Queen Margaret welcomed Sarah back with great civility, though once again Sarah was struck by her pallor and the haunted look in her eyes. She was being assailed on all sides with advice over every aspect of governing her kingdom on behalf of her small son, and the knowledge that their enemy was her own brother did nothing to alleviate the strains of her situation.

Queen Margaret had pleaded with James not to go to war with Henry, but he would not listen. His loyalty, as he told her, was to France, and when Henry took his army into France, then Scotland must go to war and stand beside her old ally.

Stand beside the new Queen of France who had been Anne, Duchess of Brittany, thought Margaret with anger in her heart. That Jezebel had flattered James and called herself his ladylove. James was full of romantic gallantry and she had been quick to assess the man. She sent him her ring with a request to march three miles into England for her sake. There had been no reasoning with James after that, thought Queen Margaret, bitterly. He had not hesitated to put the wishes of the Queen of France before the wishes of the Queen of Scotland. It was James's excuse that France had poured much-needed money into their coffers.

It was unfortunate that her husband and her brother both had fiery tempers and were expert at insulting one another, yet they had been friends for at least two years after her father, Henry VII died. But, as the Queen remembered, one of Henry's admirals had attacked two of James's ships and captured them, and she could still imagine the rage on her husband's face when Henry treated the matter as of little consequence. That had been insufferable to James, and she had known then that inevitably they would fight to the death... and that Henry would win.

When Queen Margaret was informed that a man in an azure-blue gown had commanded the King not to go to war, saying that his *mother* had commanded the King, Queen Margaret's heart had failed her. Who else could the man be but Saint John whom everyone knew was the adopted son of the Virgin Mary?

But James would not listen to the man's commandments any more than he had listened to his wife's entreaties. Now the Queen feared for his immortal soul. She had prayed for many hours on her knees, asking the Virgin Mary to forgive her husband and excuse his ignorance. Already she shuddered at the tales she had heard about what had happened to his body after Flodden.

Some said that he had retired from the kingdom and had made a pilgrimage to Jerusalem. What nonsense! Margaret knew him better than that! There was also another tale that four tall horsemen, each having a bunch of straw on the point of their spears with which to distinguish one another in the twilight, had ridden into the field at Flodden and had mounted the King on a horse and had ridden away with him.

Where had they gone? the Queen wondered. Who were the men? If that were so, then where was the King now?

Enemies of Home said he had been taken to Home Castle, where he was murdered, but Home denied this vehemently having proved himself loyal to the King.

No, Surrey had the body and the tales now reaching Margaret were even more horrific than ever, though these tales she believed to be true. John Forman and Walter Scott had wept as they identified the body of their King, and he had not received a true burial. He had been excommunicated by the Pope so that no priest would bury him in true Christian fashion. The latest news was that James's body was embalmed and lay in the monastery of Sheen in Surrey. Could this be true? Margaret wondered. She had said many prayers for his soul, but would they be heeded after he had spurned Saint John?

But now she must be strong for her son, and

only one man was beginning to soothe her fears and help to cheer her when her responsibilities threatened to break her.

The Queen tried not to think too deeply about Angus, though never before had she seen any man so handsome in his bravery. She had loved James and he, too, had been fine and brave, but he was also fiery and headstrong and her wishes had never come first with him.

But Angus was making her forget that she now bore the responsibility for the kingdom on her frail shoulders. Angus could make her heart light and bring a smile to her lips. He was a Douglas, but she had no objection to that. The Earl of Arran, who was a Hamilton, claimed kinship with them through marriage. They even proclaimed themselves royal, and Margaret frowned over this. They were no better than the Douglases in her opinion. They were certainly no better than Angus who was a prince among men. Anyone looking at him would surely think him a prince.

The trouble with being Queen Regent, thought Margaret, forlornly, was that one still had the heart of a woman.

But her son's upbringing must be carefully guarded and his well-being attended to. She was glad to welcome back Mistress Sarah Graham ... though surely she had married one of her own trusted couriers, Robin Drummond? Good. She approved of that. Mistress Sarah was a beautiful young woman, and she had caught Angus staring at the girl one day when she was last at Court. At that time she had been too concerned for James to allow this to disturb her, but now, if she were honest with herself, she did not want a rival for the attentions of Angus.

Queen Margaret examined her looks in a burnished mirror, and saw that the tired lines were beginning to leave her face and that her eyes were brighter now that she was recovering from the trauma of Flodden, and the great uncertainty in the country after James was killed. She had appealed to Henry, and he had listened, though the nobles were of the opinion that it had suited him not to pursue his advantage.

Nevertheless the wall around Edinburgh had been built and everything was done to fortify the kingdom, though the greatest of their nobles had been cut down ... except for Angus. The Queen's frozen heart was beginning to warm. He was young and very handsome, he was well-born and he cheered her where others brought nothing but misery and depression, heaping the responsibility of making decisions upon her, then grumbling if the decisions were not palatable to everyone. They would wrest the power to govern the kingdom for her son out of her hands even though James had made a will and named her specifically as his heir in trust for her son. She had to be strong for Jamie, but Angus would help. He gave her advice which made her feel that she was still the Queen Regent. He was the only one on whom she had come to depend.

* * *

Sarah met the Earl of Angus in one of the stone corridors near the nursery quarters and learned that he called each day to see that the King was well and in good health.

'To keep his claws on my wee mannie,' Lady Jane whispered to Sarah. 'I tell you, the Douglases have got their hold on the Queen and it is their word in everything nowadays. King James's temper would be at fever pitch if he could see what they were about. He was always a fiery sort of man.'

Sarah had been sent to the Great Hall to eat, and Angus was on his way to see the child. Sarah found herself staring up into his fine handsome face before she had time to draw breath.

Colour flew immediately to her cheeks and she saw the immediate response in his eyes as he put out an arm and stopped her progress.

'So it is Mistress Sarah back again,' he said with a smile. 'Rumour has it that you had married that elegant boy, young Master Drummond. I would have thought you would choose a good strong man, Mistress Sarah, one who would be a fitting partner for a handsome girl such as you have become.'

His tone was warm and teasing and his eyes roamed over her face. Sarah could not control the loud beating of her heart, yet she knew she must learn to treat Angus with the respect due to one of the highest in the land. The Douglases were a very powerful family, and in the past they had been at odds with the King because of that power, but Lady Jane had warned her well.

'Treat Angus in a circumspect fashion,' the old woman had warned, 'or the Queen Regent will not be so favourable towards you.'

Now Sarah could see that there was a new arrogance about Angus as he grinned at her. Perhaps the rumours were true. Perhaps he *was* keeping an eye on the King and was sure of his power at Court.

'Let me pass, please sir,' she said, trapped as she was by his arm.

'So soon? We have not even exchanged the time of day yet. I missed you, beautiful Sarah. Did you know that? I could see that you were growing into a great beauty and by God I was right.'

His eyes roved over her face.

'We must get to know each other a little better. I come to make regular visits to the King, and I will expect a report on his progress from you every day.'

'Lady Jane Hamilton is in charge of King James,' she said nervously.

'An old woman, soon to be in her dotage,

and a Hamilton! I have no time for the Hamiltons. No, if you give satisfaction...' He gave her a sideways glance, '... if you give satisfaction, my dear Sarah, I do not see why you cannot be in full charge of the King. It would please the Queen Regent, I am sure, and...' again his eyes flickered over her, '... it would please me.'

The colour had gone from Sarah's cheeks. There was no mistaking Angus's tones. She had not been mistaken when she was last at Court, and he *did* find her attractive.

At the same time a sense of apprehension assailed her. It was not at all prudent for her to become friends with Angus, and it was too late for her now. She was a married woman and there must be no scandal attached to the name she now bore. If any breath of scandal was heard by the Drummonds, then her position would not be good.

Besides... how did she feel now? Looking up into his bold dark eyes, she hardly knew. Angus fascinated her. She felt almost powerless in his presence and it seemed that he could command her in whatever way he chose. And something in that troubled her. She did not want to be in thrall to anyone.

'I am here to assist Lady Jane,' she said, quietly. 'I have been bidden to eat since Lady Jane remains in the nurseries. It is true that I am now married and my husband is Master Robin Drummond and he serves my father until my brother comes of age. He...'

'Was your father's choice, not yours,' said Angus, very softly. 'I am certain of that, Mistress Sarah.'

The ready colour told its own tale.

'You were wise to return to Court,' he told her in the same dulcet tones. 'We must all take up our responsibilities which can often be at odds with our desires. But there is no reason why we should not cheer one another when our duties weigh heavily on our shoulders. Go for your supper, Sarah. There is plenty of time for us to ... to talk.'

His arm remained in front of her and his eyes held hers, then he slowly pulled it away, bending swiftly to kiss her on the lips. She drew back with an intake of breath and her hand flew to her lips. She had so often dreamed of such a moment, but now that it had come, she knew fear instead of pleasure and excitement.

'You should have waited for me, little Sarah,' he whispered. 'You should not be so quick to arrange your life. I will go and see the babe. He is a precious child and I will need you to look to his good health for the Queen ... and for me.'

'I will serve the King at all times,' she said, making a great effort to compose herself with dignity. Her legs could scarcely support her as she made her way to the Great Hall. Her appetite had deserted her after her encounter with Angus, and she felt almost sick with nerves and a strange sense of foreboding about her future.

Angus was a very powerful man in every way. She could not help being so drawn to him that she was in danger of obeying his every wish. Yet there was danger in it for her. Sarah tried to clear her aching head and to use her common sense.

Several of the ladies at Court welcomed her back, as they ate supper together in the Great Hall.

Lady Mary Cunningham, one of the Queen's younger attendants, arrived late and sat down tiredly, though her eyes were bright and she was full of mischievous gossip.

'The Queen must have her hair dressed in three different styles and with three different headdresses,' she complained. 'She is never satisfied with herself, but we all know who is to blame, do we not?'

'Give your tongue a rest,' Mistress Anne Grieve, one of the older women, told her. 'She is the Queen Regent, is she not? She is a Royal Princess and is entitled to be admired, but there is no man in this kingdom good enough for a Queen, or even a Princess of the Royal Blood.'

'It has happened before,' Lady Mary shrugged. 'That is why the Hamiltons claim royal blood.'

'The nobles would not accept it,' Anne Grieve said. 'It would be her downfall.'

'But who would take her place if she did defy

the nobles?' one of the other women asked.

Lady Anne reached out a wrinkled hand for a piece of bread.

'Albany,' she said in a whisper, her eyes sweeping round for caution. 'His father was banished to France by our wee King's grandfather. He is dead now, God rest his soul, but the present duke is a fine upstanding man, or so they say, and cousin to the King. He could be Regent if the Queen makes foolish decisions. I have tried to drop a wee hint in her ear, but she will not listen, though I have served her since she came to Scotland and I love her like my own bairn.'

'But she *is* Queen Regent,' said Lady Mary.

'Aye, she is the Queen Regent by right, but Angus is swaggering about in a very arrogant fashion and the nobles cannot thole him. I detest the man myself.'

'I, too, detest him,' said Lady Mary.

'Only because he ignores your favours,' one of the other ladies put in, teasingly, and Lady Mary coloured with anger.

'He does not despoil *me*, but there are those amongst us who should be well warned.' She looked pointedly at Sarah. 'Mistress Drummond has newly arrived back at Court...'

'Aye, and she will think it a hotbed of gossip,' Anne Grieve interrupted, 'worse than in King James's time. He had hold over his Court and none of us would dare to utter a word of gossip then.'

'Well, it is a place full of gossip and unrest now,' said Lady Mary sullenly. 'You should have remained at Larraig, Graham ... I must ask pardon ... Drummond.'

Sarah said nothing. Mary Cunningham had always looked at her sullenly. In looks they were not unalike, but Sarah had grown taller and her skin glowed with colour. Her figure was superb and though her court gowns had grown shabby, they failed to disguise her beauty.

'I had thought we had enough maidservants to wash the King's linen,' Lady Mary said and again Sarah flushed. She had always been made to feel that her position in the royal household was a lowly one, but the King had demanded the best for his son, and Sarah had been proud of her position. King James had respected her grandmother, Lady Margaret, and had requested Sarah as an assistant nursemaid to his son. She had been delighted to accept the appointment, but now she made no reply. She would remain silent until she learned by her own observations how matters stood at Court.

Yet that night as she settled down to sleep knowing that she was on call in case the baby King was fretful, she tried to rest her aching head and to woo sleep which would not come. She thought about Angus, but his figure was more shadowy than that of Robin Drummond.

They had shared the same bed and his body, next to her own, had been comforting and had given her a sense of security she had never known before.

What would he say if he knew that Angus had kissed her even though she had not invited it? In her mind's eye she could see Robin's eyes turning to blue ice. He had made it very clear that she belonged to him now.

Suddenly Sarah felt cold though the bed was warm and comfortable. Drummond would not tolerate Angus casting eyes in her direction. He had made sure that their marriage was binding.

CHAPTER TEN

Angus began to pay more visits to the nursery than usual, and Lady Jane became sulky and cast sideways glances at Sarah, even though the other maidservants also blushed and bobbed a curtsey when he made his appearance.

For Sarah there was special attention, however, and when he found her alone, he would playfully pull the strings of her starched over-dress, then kiss her so that she grew agitated and pushed him away. If only things had been different, she might have welcomed his attentions because despite her good sense, she could not help finding his youth and boisterous spirits stimulating and exciting.

But soon these stolen moments were not enough for Angus and he began to whisper in her ear, inviting her to a more intimate relationship so that she grew afraid even though her blood leapt at such a thought.

As the weeks passed and he grew more insistent that his demands should be met, Sarah tried hard to avoid him. It was becoming known that he would often seek his pleasures amongst women of lesser rank and she began to realize that his attentions were degrading to her.

Lady Jane had watched her with shadowed eyes and some of the other ladies grew quiet when she went to take her place in the Great Hall. It was now well known that the Queen Regent also found Angus a stimulating companion and that he was paying court to her.

'You play with fire, Mistress,' Lady Jane told Sarah. 'The Queen has her spies. I do not trust Mary Cunningham. She has a wild look in her eyes at times and rumour has it that Angus was her lover before he gained the title and saw even greater power within his grasp.'

Sarah made no reply as she stitched at new petticoats for the little King.

'Husband to the Queen,' Lady Jane continued. 'What else but husband to the Queen.'

'Such rumours abound,' said Sarah, 'but I do not believe she would marry a man who is not a prince in his own right.'

'Oh, would she not? She is besotted, and a woman who is in thrall to a man has forgotten reason. Look at yourself, Madam! You take no heed of the sly smiles and those who laugh and point behind your back. You, too, admire him.'

Sarah stared at her, scarlet-cheeked. Lady Jane was changing and had become ill-tempered and truculent just as Angus had predicted. He had said she was not fit to be in charge of the King and truly Sarah began to wonder if he was not correct. She was a Hamilton and would always want to show the Douglases in a bad light.

'They are fools, those who speak so,' she said, hotly. 'I have done nothing wrong.'

'Only because you fear your grandmother, Lady Margaret. She was always my good friend, but truly I am no friend to her if I do not try to open your eyes to that swaggering, arrogant fool. He is handsome and brave, I grant you, but he is too young for wisdom. If he wants the Queen, he should keep his eyes on *her* and not on her ladies.'

'She has no need for concern in my case,' said Sarah with dignity.

'Nevertheless you have aroused the jealousy of Cunningham. She is strange, that one. Some said it was because of Angus, but I have heard a whisper that she is jealous of you because of Drummond.'

'Drummond! Robin!'

'Aye, Robin Drummond, your husband. He was at Court here, serving the Queen, before he returned to Larraig as squire to your father. He is a courtly gentleman, and his manners make such men as Angus look like oafs. He knows how to charm a lady and I saw Lady Mary's eyes following him with the same looks as the Queen casts on Angus, or as you sometimes cast on Angus when you think no one is looking. Oh yes, he binds you to him and twines round your heart, even if your head rejects him.'

Sarah sat down feeling sick. She had been angry before with the old woman's words, but now she felt as though she had been dealt a body blow. Robin! Robin and Lady Mary Cunningham! She had felt the other girl's animosity towards herself but she had thought it was because she was of a jealous nature and behaved in this fashion to most of the other ladies, in turn.

But to learn that she had been favoured by Robin! Sarah felt as though her world had been turned upside down. She did not *want* Robin to favour another woman. Yet she had known that he had had lovers, but she had imagined he had found his ladies in the French Court, and that they were well away from touching their lives. They had been of no consequence.

But Lady Mary was here beside her. It galled her to think of Lady Mary Cunningham even casting an eye on Robin, who was her husband.

And Lady Mary was a well-born woman.

'If Robin Drummond paid court to Lady Mary,' she said, huskily, 'why did he not wed her instead of me? It appears, if what you believe is true, that she would have been willing enough?'

'She was betrothed at that time to a Gordon and Robin was already promised to you, and you to him, as I remember. Your grandmother informed me of the match after your father arranged it. Donald Gordon did not survive Flodden and Robin gave the news to Lady Mary, though she knew it already. She screeched and scratched, but she soon rallied from her grief, that one. She was more disappointed that the knot was never tied, than that poor young Gordon fell to an English arrow.'

Lady Jane shook her head sadly.

'There will be quite a few ladies left wanting a husband,' she said. 'Our land will be decimated if our rulers do not cease their battles. At least the Queen Regent has no stomach for fighting, and she would be well to think again if she casts her eyes on Angus. Her ladies are not happy for her but she only sees jealousy in all eyes. There will be fighting amongst the nobles themselves, if he gains the power, and he is a very impatient man. He will want her to stand beside him at the altar before the King is properly cold in his grave. That will not endear her to her subjects. Take heed of my words and you will see that they are wise.'

She sighed deeply again then trotted over to the cot as the two-year-old King began to wake and howl for his supper.

'Wet through! Oh, but you are a fine lusty wee mannie. If I could but give you some years to put on you *now*, then take them off again when you reach my age, then you might have a better life. But I fear for you, my wee mannie, I fear for you. Change his wet drawers, Mistress Sarah and I will warm him with some good nourishing gruel.'

'Very well, Lady Jane,' said Sarah, forcing herself back to reality and the mundane tasks which can often be a comfort when times are troubled.

'And take care with that young woman, Mary Cunningham,' the older woman told her as a parting piece of advice. 'I do not think she is right in the head. She has a feverish light in her eyes that I have seen on people of her ilk. She will choose a bad weapon to hurt you if she has the chance. She will use Angus because I have thought the matter carefully, and it is my belief that she wishes to take Robin Drummond from you. She will know very well that he would never tolerate his wife besmirching his name and should you do so, he would petition to have the marriage annulled. After all, you have not lived together as man and wife.'

Sarah made no reply as she carried out her

duties in a mechanical fashion. They *had* lived together as man and wife but for such a short time that it might never have happened.

Yet it had happened and now her heart began to pain her for the sweetness of Robin's arms. She had thought she despised him. She had thought he was not half the man Angus was, but how wrong she had been! Robin stood up like a slender thread of gold against a mountain of copper. He was delicate in his dealings but he was strong and fine. She loved him. Such love as she had never known began to flood her heart so that she saw Angus for what he was, as clearly as she saw her own hands administering to the babe. The Queen should not marry him. He was unworthy of her, being selfish and arrogant. He did not want the Queen as a woman. He only wanted the position. He did not even love her, Sarah, and only wanted to possess her and humiliate her because he knew that she had been infatuated by his looks and had tormented herself in trying to resist his advances.

If Lady Jane had not wakened her out of her dreams, he might have succeeded in ruining her. Sarah shivered at the thought, and the last of her regard for Angus vanished as though it had never been, and revulsion took its place. How could she ever have thought him more handsome than Robin? She longed to see her husband again. If only the Queen Regent had not sent for her!

But she had desperately wanted to get away from her marriage, she reminded herself. She had left Robin in no doubt that she did not care for him and did not welcome his attentions. He would soon tire of being spurned. Perhaps already he regretted his bargain with Sir Thomas. Many younger noblemen became squires to a baron and learned how to manage an estate and how to keep it protected and steadfast against all evils, be it attack from one's enemies or from the vagaries of the weather.

But Robin had little need for such learning. He was accepting the responsibility thrust upon him because of his regard for Sir Thomas Graham. That regard had extended to marriage with his daughter, and she was a suitable match for a man in Robin's position, but it had been negotiated whilst Lady Mary was also betrothed and not free for him to approach at that time. The Cunninghams would have been glad to accept an offer from Robin Drummond. Sarah's thoughts were tormented as never before. She wanted to ride home at once to Larraig and throw herself immediately into Robin's arms asking him to think of no one but herself. But she could imagine his lips curling with scorn. It was the behaviour of just such a spoilt child as he believed her to be.

Lady Mary was older and more mature than herself and she was well-born. She also looked rather like Sarah, but many people acknowledged her to be handsome. Perhaps Robin only tolerated her because of that likeness. Perhaps every time he put his arm round his wife, his thoughts were on Lady Mary Cunningham.

Tears pricked Sarah's eyes as she carried out her tasks in the nursery and helped the maidservants to clear away the soiled clothing to the laundries where the washer-women, whose hands always looked raw and red from much scouring, would cleanse them and make them fit for the King's use once again. The Queen Regent was as fond of scrubbing as Robin Drummond and did not believe that natural sweats kept illness at bay.

'I only give warning, child,' said Lady Jane, coming to touch her cheek where a tear had trickled down from Sarah's brimming eyes. The sudden clarity of her emotions had caused her heart to swell as though it would fill her throat and she swallowed to remove the lump. Tears cascaded down her cheeks.

'I do not love Angus,' she whispered. 'I only want my ... my husband.'

'He is worth your tears, the other is not. Now, it is time to play with the wee mannie so dry your eyes and all will be well. You will take care from now on, of that I am sure and I thank God for it because I am fond of you, child. Now our precious charge must learn to play, else he has sorrow on him all his life and will not know where it comes from. Everyone needs their childhood, Sarah.'

CHAPTER ELEVEN

Sarah felt that she had opened Pandora's box as more and more happenings began to plague her. She had sighed with heartfelt relief when Angus was obliged to leave Court in order to deal with troubles on one of his estates. He had been able to look to his grandfather, Bell-the-Cat to see that the properties were well run and brought in good revenues, and had expected that his father or uncle would take their share of responsibility.

But Flodden had thrown the full weight of that responsibility on to his shoulders and he had neglected his affairs, preferring to stay close to the Queen. He had inherited the Douglas love of power, and saw that whoever was in charge of the King's person could surely hold that power. How better to gain control of the child than to marry the Queen.

Angus had been brought up to believe that the powerful family of Douglas was equal to any Stewart, though his ancestors had lost their lives, or had been banished for holding such beliefs. Now he believed himself good enough, if not too good, for the widowed

Queen, even if she were sister to the King of England!

Some of his property on the Borders had been ravished by the English soldiers as they marched into Scotland, and Angus gathered his men together and rode south.

Sarah was more than happy to see him go. The weather had become warmer and the Queen decreed that her son should have a short spell of fresh air each day, much to the foreboding of Lady Jane. Sarah was given the responsibility of wrapping him up in his velvets and soft woollens, and taking him to play in a quiet corner of the courtyard, well guarded by soldiers.

Angus had dismissed the guard one day on his own authority, saying he would be responsible to the Queen for the King's safety, and reluctantly the soldiers had left, knowing that Angus was a favourite with the Queen.

He had lost little time when he and Sarah were left alone, and immediately pulled her down to sit on his plaid and began to make love to her with an almost feverish look in his eyes.

'You are becoming more and more beautiful to me, Sarah Graham,' he said, thickly. 'We are not given sufficient opportunities to be alone together.'

'I do not seek to be alone with you, sir,' she said, panting as she pulled away from him. There was the smell of wine on his breath and the flush of drunkenness on his cheeks, 'and I am Mistress Drummond, sir, not Graham.'

'A poor match, as I say, my Sarah. You and I could do well together. You need the love of a real man, but there is so little time. Give the child that ball and come under my plaid with me.'

'No!' she cried, horrified, 'it is more than my life is worth, and I would not do so, sir, because I do not love you and I respect my husband. His name will not be besmirched by me.'

'You are grown very high and mighty, Madam,' said Angus, 'and if I did not know you fear the Queen, I might believe your arguments. But I know that you have love for me. I have seen it in your eyes. Come now, do not be shy and waste time for us. The child will soon tire of his ball.'

He began to push at her skirts and in a panic she struggled feverishly, afraid to call out lest she would be blamed for enticing him, but she fought him silently, knowing that she had little chance against his great strength.

Then the child ran towards them and a moment later his lip trembled and he began to howl. Angus looked round at him and Sarah managed to pull herself away and smooth down her clothing. She grabbed the child into her arms.

'Sir, you would not harm the King,' she said in a low furious voice. 'I am asking you to allow us to go.'

'Nor would I harm you, you stupid creature,' he told her, dusting down his own coat. His eyes glittered with anger as he looked at her and she knew that there was very real fear of him in her heart. How could she have thought herself in love with him!

'No woman denies me, not even the highest in the land,' he told her. 'If I want you, I shall have you, Madam. But for now the mood has left me. Now go and attend to your duties. It is too cold for King James to be out of doors and he will be chilled.'

She clasped the child to her thankfully, and hurried along the cold stone corridors to the nursery quarters, hoping no one would see her until she had changed out of her torn and soiled clothing, and re-arranged her cap over her tangled hair. She imagined that she heard a faint smothered cry, but when she looked around, she could see no one and wasted no further time.

In her own bedchamber she changed her clothing and hid her torn garments so that she could mend them before giving them to the washerwoman. Her head ached and she felt sick and ill.

Lady Jane offered to excuse her duties for the rest of the day when she saw Sarah's white face and distressed eyes, but the younger woman shook her head. She felt a great cold rage gathering inside her. Why should she hide herself away? She had done nothing wrong. Why should she hide like some poor slave girl, from the Earl of Angus. She was no light-skirt to be used carelessly and thrown aside, and in any case, she had managed to fight for her virtue, and to win. She was the daughter of Graham of Larraig and the wife of Drummond.

'I will go to supper as usual,' she told Lady Jane, 'though my head aches and I am not myself.' She had a glint in her eyes which made the old woman speculate. She did not know how to read Mistress Sarah these days, but the girl trod a dangerous path. Something had upset and distressed her and Lady Jane's mind was shrewd and discerning. It would be better for Sarah to return to her home at Larraig.

But she needed Sarah, thought Lady Jane. She was equally vulnerable herself. Angus swaggered and postured and everyone looked on him with suspicion, but his would be the power at Court one of these fine days, with King James scarcely cold in his grave ... if he was in his grave? Some were not completely certain. Only two of his men had seen his body.

Suppose, as some suggested, he had gone on a pilgrimage to the Holy Land, to do penance for marching his men out at Flodden Field, then he would return to them one of these days. Now *that* would be a fine thing for my Lord Angus!

The King sneezed and Lady Jane rushed to cosset him.

'The air is too cold and damp for my wee man,' she told Sarah whose cheeks were once again flushing painfully. She had been forced to leave the King when it would have been more practical to make the child run round and keep warm. But at any rate she had not been besmirched by the man whom she now loathed. She would not be ashamed to look Robin in the eye when they met again.

*   *   *

Angus was called away to his Border estates. Before leaving Court he had a private interview with the Queen who emerged with a hint of fever in her eyes and a deep excitement alternating with depression which was a great trial to her ladies. Lady Mary Cunningham was scolded several times and went into a sullen mood, her eyes following Sarah whenever their paths crossed. Sarah hardly noticed. She was worried about the King who had developed a cough which strained his small body and which did not respond to Lady Jane's home-brewed remedies.

'We must have the physician,' said Sarah, fearfully. 'He will know what to do for the King.'

Had the child caught a chill when Angus forced her to be neglectful of him?

'He will preach heresy more likely,' said Lady Jane. 'It is all one hears these days. Every physician is trying to heal the soul as well as the body, and making a poor job of both.'

'He can heal the King's soul if he wishes,' said Sarah, 'but he must also make the King well. These men devote their lives to studying cures for sickness.'

She begged audience with the Queen who looked at her with veiled eyes so that Sarah was in no doubt that the rumours that Angus was favouring her had reached the ears of the Queen.

'How has my son come to sicken with this illness?' she asked, though immediately she rose and cancelled any further audiences. 'You and Lady Jane are engaged to ensure that he does not take any harm, Mistress Drummond. I hope you have not been careless with his person and have, maybe, spent some of your time attending to ... to personal matters?'

'No, Madam,' said Sarah, quickly. 'Please believe that I am devoted to the King. I ... I love him.'

Surely he could not have caught this illness through neglect in such a short time!

The Queen softened a little, aware of the sincerity in the girl's voice.

'I believe you do, Drummond, but ... ah ... certain matters can make one forget one's *own* well-being, and also that of another in one's charge. Do you understand me?'

'I understand, Madam, but please believe that there is no one in Court whose interests I would serve higher than those of the King.'

'I would hope that is so,' the Queen

said, coldly.

Swiftly she walked towards the nursery and bent over the child who looked heavy-eyed and whose cheeks were flushed with high colour.

'He has caught a fever,' the Queen said, crisply. 'I shall order the physician to attend to him, but I am not satisfied, Lady Jane, with your attendance on him, neither am I satisfied with Mistress Drummond even though your husband serves me well. We will see what the physician has to say.'

'Aye, Madam, and grieved we will be if the wee man is not better by tomorrow,' said Lady Jane.

Her head shook as she bent over the cot, and Sarah felt a pang of dismay as she looked at the old woman attending to the sleeping child. Lady Jane looked suddenly very old and frail. She would not be able to depend on her to nurse the child well again, and Sarah's heart filled with renewed fears. Suppose ... suppose the King's chill *had* been caused by being left to kick a ball whilst she tried to fight off the advances of Angus ... what then? The soldiers knew that Angus had sent them away and could well hazard a guess as to why he wanted to be alone with Sarah. Should she confess to the Queen? But if she did so, she would be obliged to accept all the blame, and Angus would receive none of it. Sarah felt a stirring of anger again. It had been none of *her* doing. She had *not* invited his attentions.

The physician arrived and examined the child, then left medicines which he claimed would improve his condition, but the fever ran high in the King's small body and, filled with guilt, Sarah helped to nurse him night and day, taking over from Lady Jane whenever the old woman felt too tired to carry on. She remembered her grandmother's recipes for chills and fevers and sponged the child's head and arms with a mixture of boiled waters and various herbs. She was glad when the tiny boy could not swallow the noxious brew which Lady Jane prepared.

She grew tired and light-headed with her worries and anxieties, and paid little heed to those around her, though she was happy to receive a message from Larraig with greetings from her father, Sir Thomas. He was now well recovered from his wounds, but it had gone ill once more for Robin's brother, recently married, but ill of his fevers. Robin had ridden home to help attend to the affairs of the Drummonds.

One of the other ladies had heard the news from Larraig, and looked slyly at Sarah.

'You did well to choose Master Drummond as a husband, who manages to wriggle free of the weapons wielded by his enemies, for I hear he bears not a scratch,' she said, lightly. 'Now his brother is sick of his wounds. I tell you, our Mistress Sarah will yet be a countess!'

Sarah flushed angrily.

'I do not care whether I am a countess or a cotter,' she said, defiantly. 'I am myself and nothing else matters.'

'Except bringing the King back to health,' Lady Mary Cunningham said, her eyes glittering, 'though it appears that you tell us a fine tale, Mistress Drummond. If you had not been so low-born, you would have lifted your eyes to Angus. As it is, you made do with Drummond who is too good for you. But if he becomes heir at Balwhidden, then best look out, Mistress, for some of us might not care to see you placed above us at table.'

'I tell you, I care nothing for such things,' said Sarah, 'and it is true that I only care to restore the King to health.'

'And we know why, do we not?' asked Lady Mary, very softly, though her eyes were malevolent.

Sarah shivered. The older girl did not look quite sane at times. What could she have in mind? Had she seen Angus trying to force her that day? But if so, why had she not spoken? If she wanted to do Sarah harm, then she only had to whisper a word in the Queen's ear. Again Sarah shivered and felt almost sick at the thought.

But perhaps Lady Mary was more prudent. After all, Angus also was implicated, and if she accused Sarah, she also accused Angus. Perhaps that was why she had kept quiet all the time.

But Lady Jane had warned her to be wary of Mary Cunningham. It was Robin whom she wanted, not Angus. Now she imagined that his prospects had altered with this bad news about his brother, and there was even more reason for Lady Mary to resent her.

Sarah's heart was heavy for Robin's brother, his new wife and his parents. Surely, however, the news which had been recounted to her so carefully assured her that it was only a temporary lapse and that all would be well with her brother-in-law after his wounds had again been dressed by the physician. He was not sick to his death, and Sir Neil was still a fine strong man. Lady Mary was trying to taunt her for her own purposes. She was bored at Court, which still mourned the death of the King, and was dull in her opinion. She found her amusement in pestering Sarah.

Had she and Robin been lovers? Sarah wondered, jealously, as the harsh taste of it filled her mouth. She could not bear to think of Robin in this woman's arms. She was like a witch, thought Sarah, shivering, and witches had their own ways of accomplishing what they wanted.

But she would have welcomed a message from Robin. She would have welcomed a small sign that he looked on her as his true wife and had a fondness for her.

But she had spurned him before they left Larraig, she remembered. She had shown contempt for him when she now recognized that he was the bravest and ablest of men.

She had been taunted that he had not earned himself a scratch, but his lack of wounds was a mark in his favour and not something to be deplored. Robin was neat and agile. He delivered more blows than he collected by his skill in using his lithe body to his best advantage. She had defended him roundly so that she found Lady Mary's eyes on her with new intelligence, and later the older girl had come after her.

'So you love him after all,' she said, softly. 'You see the worth of the man you married. You are a nobody compared with him, and he has a heart too big for you to comprehend, but though I pleaded with him not to sacrifice himself, his honour was too great to renege from the contract.'

Sarah's step faltered, and slowly she turned to listen.

'I do not know what you mean,' she said, though her heart was beating uncomfortably.

'Do you not? Why should you? You were not important enough to be consulted. You were merely the pawn in the game.' She smiled again, but her eyes shone with hatred and jealousy.

'Your father saved the life of Sir Neil Drummond when they fought together for our child-King's grandfather. The Drummonds and the Grahams had always been enemies, or are you not even aware of that?'

Oh yes, she knew that! thought Sarah, afraid of what she would learn next, yet powerless to walk away without listening.

'So the old enemies became friends as has often happened in the past. The old King, James the Third, had favourites and neither Graham nor Drummond supported those favourites, any more than did the grandfather of Angus, Archibald Bell-the-Cat. That formed a bond between them.'

'So...?'

'So when they rode to Flodden, Robin was commanded by Sir Neil to ride close to Sir Thomas Graham. There was a debt to pay. Robin paid that debt by saving your father when he might have been left to rot on the field.'

Sarah listened and remembered how her father had clung to Robin, even after they returned to Larraig. He had treated him like a son even before he had told her that a match had been arranged between them.

Lady Mary was watching her closely.

'You know it is the truth,' she said, silkily. 'There was no need to discharge the duty further by marrying you. I say the debt was discharged when Robin rode away from Flodden Field with your father in his charge. He had done enough to pay the debt owed by the Earl. But the match had already been arranged, so he was chivalrous enough to go through with it.'

Sarah felt almost physically sick.

'How do you know this?' she asked Mary Cunningham huskily. 'It is not your affair, so why should you concern yourself?'

'How else should I know other than from Robin himself? He wanted me. Aye, he wanted me desperately, but he was promised to you who are little better than the daughter of a farmer, both in looks and in the duties you undertake. You are too flamboyant in style to be a lady.'

'He could have been free had he spoken,' cried Sarah.

She did not care what Lady Mary said about her looks, but she cared very much if Robin had wanted Lady Mary instead of herself. That was almost too great a pain to bear. She did not care about the ladies in France who might have been part of his life in the past, but Lady Mary was part of her present life.

'There were other obstacles,' Mary said, and sighed heavily. 'He was a younger son. My father would not have it and the King would not give his permission. I even petitioned the Queen but she would not interfere with any judgement of this kind made by the King. Robin was a fine messenger for her. He is quick and light, and he can ride like a demon. He can deliver an urgent message in half the time it takes most messengers.'

Lady Mary's eyes shone with a feverish light.

'They would not have it, and Robin would not have me because he was already promised, to you. They would not speak for me, and he would not listen. And to think that it was merely Graham's daughter ... you! He had paid the debts of his father, and the price had been heavy. But he made me pay the price as well as himself, and I owe the Grahams nothing.'

'I do not believe all of this,' said Sarah, painfully.

'It matters not whether you believe it, or whether you do not. Now the real tragedy of our lives may well be upon us. If his brother dies, Robin is heir to Balwhidden and a fitting partner for a Cunningham. But already he has taken you to wife, so we will have to wait until he is free of you, Mistress Sarah.'

Her voice had dropped to a whisper and she began to laugh, low and deep in her throat, so that Sarah felt more frightened than ever before. Surely Lady Mary Cunningham was an unstable creature. Perhaps the fact that she had lost Drummond had unbalanced her. She stared at the laughing face with horror, then as suddenly the laughter had gone.

'You will not stand in the way of happiness,' she said, her eyes now hard as stones. 'I tell you, he loves me and only me. You are only a poor shadowy picture of myself. That is why he thought he could tolerate you. But he cannot. I know he cannot. Soon he will want to be free of you and all you stand for. Soon he will see that he owes Larraig nothing.'

'You have said enough to me,' said Sarah, gathering her wits about her though she felt more afraid than she had ever been in her life. She felt as though a rock on which she had built her life was suddenly crumbling beneath her feet.

*   *   *

Lady Jane looked at her white face when she returned to the nursery and ordered her to lie down for an hour or two.

'One of the maidservants will watch over the King,' she said. 'He is sleeping, though his fever still runs high. The sweat will not break on him, not even with my potions.'

'I will watch over him,' said Sarah. 'No one else will take care of him but ourselves, Lady Jane.'

She could not rest until she knew that the King was out of danger.

CHAPTER TWELVE

The summer had been late in arriving and there were snell winds blowing through the streets of Edinburgh. Then suddenly the weather grew warm and the rain clouds hung over the capital so that mists blew in from the sea and shrouded the castle like the gossamer folds of one of the Queen's robes.

Soon the sun would disperse the mists, but as Sarah looked out from the nursery window, it seemed as though the mists encompassed her own life.

She had received no more news from Larraig and she longed to be free of her service to the Queen and to return home again to the warmth and shelter of her family. Desperately she wanted to see Robin again, though she was half-fearful of the look she would see reflected in his eyes when she questioned him about Lady Mary Cunningham. Because she would never be able to live with him happily unless she knew the truth of the matter from Robin's own lips.

At first she scarcely heard Lady Mary's screams as she ran down the corridor, but one of the maidservants had thrown open the door and had gone to investigate their cause. A few moments later she returned, hurrying along the gloomy darkness of the stone corridor with fear and alarm in her face.

'It is Lady Mary Cunningham,' she said, needlessly.

'We have ears, child,' Lady Jane said, impatiently. 'Has she been savaged by one of the dogs? She is making enough noise for it. I cannot think she would make as much noise were she savaged by one of the soldiers.'

'She has seen the ... the man in the blue gown with the yellow hair,' the girl whispered, fearfully, 'the same as appeared to King James to ask him not to go to battle before Flodden Field. She says she saw him in his azure-blue gown, just like before, and he was lit up like a saint. He only comes when a warning must be given. She was screaming that she must see the Queen at once to warn her, or the King's life may be threatened, just as it was before.'

The blood drained from Sarah's cheeks. Deep instinct told her that this boded ill for herself, though she was yet unsure as to why this was so. The man could only be Saint John again, and the fact that he had appeared to the King and he had not heeded his warning was now talked about in whispers in many a corner.

Lady Mary's vision was certainly sure to alarm the Queen Regent, and if it were truly Saint John, then fear for the King again clawed at Sarah's heart. If only she felt herself to be entirely free of guilt, she could face everyone bravely and defend the King's health with all the powers she could muster.

She had prayed fervently every day, on her knees in chapel, but would God listen to her when she had spent time in fighting Angus instead of trying with all her might to ensure that the little boy had not splashed in puddles of water, or torn off his plaid when the winds grew fierce?

'I will take my punishment,' Sarah had prayed, 'but I pray to the Holy Virgin to spare our King.'

Now that same Holy Virgin had sent Saint John to warn them once more, and this time the King himself could not be warned of danger. Only those in charge of the King's person could be warned.

Yet would Saint John be sent with such a warning? Sarah wondered. When he last appeared to King James, there was an earnest purpose behind that visitation. If King James had heeded the warning, then thousands of lives could have been saved. Five thousand English soldiers and twice that many of their own Scottish men, soldiers, noblemen, men of all trades who had gone to serve their King. They would be alive now and happy with their families had that warning been heeded.

Sarah could understand the importance of such a messenger being sent to talk to the King at his devotions, but it was a strange matter that Saint John should appear once again when the King was only a babe and not yet ready to make decisions in government. Surely the chill he had caught was not so grave. Already he was recovering from his fevers and the cooling sponge of clear water sprinkled with herbs had cooled his head and his blood. Already Lady Jane was feeding him tiny drops of chicken broth and was prophesying that he would be leaving his cot within a day.

So what else could threaten the King, or his people? If the people were threatened, then the Visitation should be made to the Queen and not to Lady Mary.

So Sarah pondered even as she returned to her duties, but Lady Jane Hamilton was silent and withdrawn as she, too, tended the King and tended to glance unhappily at Sarah even as she brooded whilst mending the bed linen. The King's small feet kicked it into shreds unless a tear was mended immediately.

'There is evil afoot,' said Lady Jane. 'I can sense it. All is not well with us and the Queen should listen to warnings, even if the King did not. It is her duty to govern our country with the help of wise men and advisers, and she should put her own desires aside in the interests of her people ... our people ... and her son.'

She shook her head and muttered a prayer.

'It is hard for a lass like her,' she said, almost to herself. 'She was never a bairn. She had to be a woman before she was grown to womanhood, and now she would have love from any handsome man whether he be suitable or not. But the people will not stand for that. The Stewarts are our anointed Kings, and no family, however powerful, will be recognized by God as the ruling family, not even Arran who is my own kinsman, unless it is the Stewart family. If Saint John has come to warn her, she should listen.'

* * *

The Queen Regent was finding that the responsibilities being heaped upon her were almost too great to bear. She was expected to govern the country on behalf of her son, yet every nobleman appeared to her to be conscious of his own personal power and demanded that his wishes be heard and acted upon. It was more than one woman could stand, she thought, as she paced the floor and tried to deal with the latest petitions.

Nor was she given respite when the chaos of the day was over, and she rested her head upon her pillow. It was then that she wrestled with her growing love for Angus, and wondered if she dared take him as her husband. How would the other nobles react? Queen Margaret shivered as though she could already hear the outcry against her.

It was not yet a year since she had lost James at Flodden Field, yet already another man filled her heart and mind. He was young and so handsome that her heart beat fast enough to suffocate her every time he returned to Court, and she felt lost and lonely when he grew cool with her for being unable to make up her mind, and returned to his estates for a few weeks. This was to give her time for thought, but she knew that it was also to instil fear into her heart that he should cast his eyes on some well-born lady who, though not a queen, would one day find favour with him.

But he was ambitious. He had made no secret of the fact, and sometimes she realized that part of her hesitation stemmed from the fact that he did not love her as much as she loved him. He admired other women. Especially he admired Mistress Sarah Drummond. The Queen fought down her jealousy. She had been reluctant to invite Mistress Sarah back to Court, but Lady Jane Hamilton had requested her presence to help with the King, and Angus had pointed out that the Grahams and the Drummonds were well-respected names among the nobles and had no quarrels with their neighbours. No one would object to a Graham looking after the child. Envy and jealousy seemed to lurk in every corner, thought Queen Margaret, and was ready to pounce if she made a move which did not meet with universal approval.

Peace was being negotiated between England and France, and she wanted Scotland to be part of the treaty to be signed shortly. The country could not afford another war, as she well knew, and some of the nobles were wise enough to see that she was a great asset to the country in that Henry of England was her own brother.

Yet others pointed out that it had made no difference when they fought at Flodden. Henry had not scrupled to throw the might of his forces against them.

Some of the nobles were already talking, as had been whispered to her, about asking John, Duke of Albany, to return from France. He had been cousin to James and in the opinion of quite a few of the nobles, he was close enough to the King to stand as Regent. His could be a stronger hand in the government of the country, and if she married Angus, she would run the risk of being banished and John put in her place. She might even lose authority over her son, thought Queen Margaret, and she was determined to safeguard her place in the country and would not tolerate the arrival of Albany.

Which meant more to her? Angus or Jamie? It was an unfair question because she loved both of them in different ways and was capable of deep passion for both.

Yet if she married Angus, it would seem to the people of her country that she was handing over the care of her son to the Douglases. That family would then most certainly become the most powerful in the country and there were those who distrusted the Douglases.

No, it would not be a popular marriage, but Queen Margaret could not dismiss Angus from her mind and heart so easily. She loved him. She was jealous of any lady who caught his attention. She wanted him and there were times when she cared nothing about the consequences.

Lady Mary Cunningham sought audience

with the Queen on a private matter, and it was granted immediately. News of her vision of Saint John had newly reached the Queen's ears and she had been about to send for Lady Mary to question her.

The girl came into her private room, looking white and apprehensive and bobbed a deep curtsey to Queen Margaret. The Queen could not decide whether or not she liked Lady Mary. Sometimes she thought that the girl had a sly sleepy look in her eyes and she reminded Queen Margaret of a cat; beautiful, elegant and in constant care of her own person.

'What is this I hear?' Queen Margaret asked. 'Visions? Saint John? Surely we are not about to start another war, Lady Mary. There has already been too much talk of Saint John in sly corners where the gossipers thought they could not be overheard. They have yet to learn that I have very keen ears!'

'I know nothing of war, Madam,' said Lady Mary, keeping her bold eyes on the floor. 'I can only say that he appeared to me in the corridor nearest to the nurseries where the King is cared for by ... by the nursing maids.'

'Lady Jane Hamilton. If Saint John brings a warning, then why should we be concerned about Lady Jane? She is an old woman and has much experience in rearing royal children.'

'She is not alone in the nurseries, Madam. There is also Mistress Sarah Drummond and she is not so experienced as Lady Jane.'

'She serves us well,' the Queen said, quickly. 'She managed to look after the King well when he was still Prince James, and a helpless babe.'

'Aye, but ... but maybe she thinks, at times, about her own affairs.'

'What affairs?'

Suddenly Lady Mary was afraid. The Queen had changed in the past year. She had grown older and harder with the affairs of office and one could not guess her reactions to certain matters. Problems which had irritated her at one time she now shrugged off as being insignificant, but others brought a burst of rage similar to those rages attributed to her brother, King Henry of England. One should never forget that she was an English Princess.

'She is not to be trusted with the King's person,' said Lady Mary, sulkily. She did not like the Queen's tones, as though she, herself, were in the wrong.

'Why do you say so?'

'She is too ... too wayward ...'

The Queen sighed and stared hard at the other girl.

'Explain yourself, Lady Mary. This is a serious matter. If you have knowledge which I do not have, then it is your duty to speak. If you keep such knowledge to yourself then it may do harm to you in the future.'

Lady Mary's eyes showed a hint of fear.

'I ... I did not come to you because the man she dallied with is of high rank and is esteemed by ... by yourself, Madam.'

'Which man? What are you trying to say?'

Lady Mary ran a tongue over her dry lips.

'Before the King caught the chill, Madam, Mistress Sarah took him into the fresh air, then left him whilst she dallied with ... with my lord, the Earl of Angus.'

The last name was spoken almost in a whisper and Lady Mary began to regret that she had spoken at all when she saw the Queen's face contorted with anger.

'How do you know that she dallies with Angus?' she asked, tightly. 'Why do you accuse her?'

'I saw them,' Lady Mary whispered.

'Them!'

'Her. It was she who ... who was at fault. They were in the courtyard where ... where the King is allowed to play. They were ... together ... under his plaid ... whilst the King played alone and splashed his feet in cold water. She neglected her charge, and now he is ill.'

'And you said nothing!'

Queen Margaret rose with blazing eyes and her face was so white that Lady Mary could have fainted at the sight of her.

'You said nothing ... nothing!'

'I ... I was afraid, Madam. I ... I fear she is a witch. How else could she bring herself to the notice of Angus, and ... and capture Drummond so that he is forced into marriage.'

So it is Drummond with Lady Mary,

thought the Queen as she listened to the change of tone. Her own anger cooled a little as she noted the feverish light in the other woman's eyes. She began to have sympathy in her heart for Lady Mary Cunningham as she looked more closely at her tortured face. It was hard to love a man with great passion, and see him dangling after another woman.

And it was Sarah Graham who had ensnared both men! She would have to take action against the girl immediately. *Had* she been responsible for the King's illness? Already he was recovering from his chill, but if Mistress Graham or Drummond as she now was, had brought it on by neglect, then it was a treasonable offence and could only be punished by death.

But she could not condemn the young woman without trial, and if there was a trial, then Angus would be implicated. If she hoped to present Angus to her people as a true husband for herself, and a powerful help in governing the country, then this sort of scandal would not be helpful. It required a great deal of thought.

'You may go,' she said to Lady Mary. 'There is much to be considered. Say nothing to anyone about this conversation and no word of it to Mistress Drummond, or it will be the worse for you, Cunningham. Do you understand?'

'Yes, Madam.'

Lady Mary Cunningham made her escape and the Queen paced her chamber restlessly, trying to marshal her thoughts, and to make the best decision possible, It might be one crucial to her whole future.

CHAPTER THIRTEEN

It was two days before the Queen Regent sent for Sarah and when one of the guards came to find her instead of a boy page, her heart bounded with terror. Despite Queen Margaret's warning. Lady Mary Cunningham had been unable to keep quiet about her audience with the Queen and the other ladies began to look askance at Sarah, and there were few who still wanted to remain close to her in friendship.

The reputation of the Queen's brother, Henry VIII of England, for uncertain fiery tempers and the speedy removal of those who stood in his way, was well known at the Scottish Court and the Queen Regent's temper was also suspect. She well knew, however, that her authority was much less certain than that of her brother and she was therefore obliged to move with more care.

But the word 'neglect' of the King's person, and 'treason' had been whispered amongst the ladies and even Lady Jane Hamilton had remained quiet and furtive as they worked together in the nursery where the King was now almost fully recovered from his chill.

Sarah dropped a deep curtsey when she was shown into the presence of the Queen, but when she dared to look up into Queen Margaret's face, her heart beat painfully with apprehension. At the same time, the fierce pride which had always been hers began to stiffen her backbone. If anyone were to be put on trial for neglecting the King, it should be Angus. She had been forcibly held by him so that she could not attend to the King's person. She had not wanted any attention from Angus.

'It has been brought to my notice that you dallied with the Earl of Angus when you should have given your full attention to my son,' Queen Margaret said, icily. 'Is this true, Mistress Drummond?'

'I had no choice, Madam,' Sarah said, quietly. 'My Lord Angus made a prisoner of me. I could not attend to the King because he held me back from him.'

'Liar!' the Queen hissed. 'You would try to put the blame for your own failure on to another person. It is not the responsibility of the Earl of Angus to nurse my son. That responsibility was given to you, mistakenly, as I now believe since you have proved yourself untrustworthy. For your neglect, I should have given orders to throw you into the dungeons to await trial and execution, but the Earl of

Angus is a young, handsome man and we all know that men enjoy a dalliance with a light of love.'

'I am no light of love, Madam!' Sarah cried. 'I am newly wed and ... and love my husband dearly.'

'That is not how I heard it from Lady Jane Hamilton. It seemed that you wanted to be free of Larraig in order to avoid the marriage with Drummond. Was she so mistaken?'

Sarah's face had gone scarlet, but now the blood drained from her cheeks as she saw that her own actions had prepared a trap for herself.

'I ... she was not mistaken then, Madam, but ... but since ...'

'You appear to be in some doubt as to what you *do* want, Mistress Drummond,' the Queen said, icily. 'It was also told to me that you admired Angus very much on the last occasion of your service at Court.'

'No longer, Madam,' said Sarah, fervently. 'I do not admire him. I think he is conceited and ... and swaggering and thinks he may have any woman ...'

She broke off biting her lip at the expression on the Queen's face.

'Indeed?' Margaret asked, very softly, and this time Sarah's heart seemed to pound like a great stone in her breast as she saw the fury in the Queen's eyes. Too late she remembered that Angus had a special place in Queen

Margaret's affections and that perhaps Lady Jane had been quite correct in saying that the Queen was in love with him, and may even marry him!

But the Queen Regent could surely not marry such a man, thought Sarah. He was not a good enough consort for her, and he most certainly should not be allowed to have influence over the King. It would mean that the country would be governed by the Douglases.

'You will be taken to a small chamber where you will remain by yourself until I decide what must be done with you,' Queen Margaret told her icily. 'You will not return to the nurseries or have anything further to do with my son. Your work here is finished.'

Again fear swept over Sarah. She would virtually be a prisoner in the castle. She would see no one, and her meals would be served to her in the chamber.

The guard conducted her along several dark stone corridors, then she was locked into a small dark room almost bare of furniture, and very cold and dark despite the warmer weather.

Sarah lay down on the miserable uncomfortable bed and cried until she had no tears left.

* * *

Sarah began to lose count of the days as the

time passed so slowly that she felt every day to be an eternity. Food was brought to her but her questions remained unanswered and she had no appetite for her meat, though she was wise enough to know that unless she ate, her bodily strength would diminish.

Her mind also needed nourishment or it seemed to her that madness would continue to stalk her dreams. She would fall asleep through sheer exhaustion, then awake screaming with horror as she dreamed that she was being buried alive.

To counter this terror, she repeated the nursery rhymes her grandmother had taught her, and the fairy tales she had recounted to King James as she lulled him to sleep at nights. She missed his small warm body cradled in her arms, and began to daydream that she would waken soon, in her own chamber at Larraig and that she and Robin would settle down to a normal marriage and have their own children to bring them joy and hope for the future.

But the dank grey walls of the chamber, which was not a prison but a room in which she was imprisoned, soon dulled her spirits and her wits. How long must she be kept here before the Queen Regent decided on her future? How long must she await the Queen's Pleasure?

* * *

Sarah was sleeping when the guard opened the

door of her chamber and ushered in her visitor. She woke fearfully, then her face grew radiant with joy and she cried out with relief and happiness. Robin stood before her, an elegant figure in black velvet trimmed with silver. His grace and charm were almost too great for her to bear as she looked at him, and wondered why she had not known all through the years that it was Robin she loved with all the passion at her command.

'Oh, Robin!' she cried, tears making rivulets down her cheeks. She had been given very little water in which to freshen her person and she required to remove the dirt and dust from her face. 'Oh Robin, how glad I am to see you. I am full of joy that you have come.'

She would have thrown herself into his arms, but he stepped away from her and gazed stonily.

'Are these all your belongings, Mistress Drummond?' he asked, coldly, showing her some baggage. 'If so, we will be gone before the Queen Regent changes her mind and demands your life.'

Relief made her want to laugh and cry at the same time. She did not blame her fastidious Robin from avoiding her. She would need to be well scrubbed before he wanted to hold her close, even though Anna Hyslop would give her dire warnings about bathing more than four times a year.

His tone, however, was almost

contemptuous and she wondered if this was being adopted for the benefit of the guard.

'Am I being sent home under your care?' she asked. 'Oh Robin, I do not care how I go, so long as I get away from this place.'

'I thought that might be so,' he told her, heavily. 'Here is a cloak to cover yourself, and my men are waiting with horses so that we can leave at once for Larraig.'

'I cannot believe that you have come at last. I am so happy to see you.' She was laughing helplessly with hysterical relief, and hardly knew what she was saying.

'Hold your tongue!' he commanded, roughly. 'I do not think you understand the enormity of the disgrace you have brought upon your family ... and mine! ... for you bear our name and may one day be Countess of Balwhidden. If you make any more noise, Madam, I shall feel obliged to cut a switch and beat sense and decorum into you.'

The words, uttered almost venomously by Robin Drummond, seemed to lacerate her more than any which the Queen had used. Now that they were walking in bright sunshine she could see that his face was hard as granite, and that his blue eyes were like pieces of blue ice instead of the warm brightness of sapphires.

'You do not understand,' she whispered, her voice almost lost with nerves. 'They accused me falsely. I have done nothing wrong.'

'Nothing wrong! You neglected your duties,

dallied with a man most favoured by the Queen, even if he is a dunderhead, and ... and exposed the King's person to illness and disease by your own stupidity, as you have admitted. Could you not see that he was always too ambitious to treat you honourably? Cannot you tell when a man is worthless or when he values you?'

He strode ahead of her.

'You are no longer of much value, are you, Mistress Drummond?' he asked, 'but you bear my name and the name of my family, therefore I am responsible for you. I have promised the Queen that I shall take you back to Larraig, and into seclusion so that she need never set eyes on you again. Come here. Up with you.'

He helped her mount her horse though the tears were blinding her to everything else. She had so longed to see Robin again, yet this hard, harsh man was not the man she had pictured in her dreams.

'And to encourage Angus where you could be watched by Mary Cunningham! What common sense! What wit! What guile! I declare you are as stupid as Angus himself.'

She said nothing. Her voice would have been thick with tears and it was useless to argue with Robin Drummond when he was in this mood.

Then he lapsed into silence and it seemed to Sarah that the silence was worse than his scathing comments as they rode out of Edinburgh and turned towards Larraig. More and more she was conscious of her dishevelled appearance, and her lack of attraction. She had lost Robin. He despised her now and it did not matter whether she was innocent or guilty, he had no love for her and their marriage would be a sham from now on. Perhaps he would make an appeal to have the marriage annulled since they were only bedded but once, and he could deny that their marriage was consummated. Would he be hard enough to take such a step? Perhaps he would put her away from him, whatever happened, and no one would blame him. If he appealed to the Queen Regent, she would listen with sympathy.

It would have been expedient for him to leave her in Edinburgh, thought Sarah. Her life was a prison to her now, as much a prison as that terrible room she had left behind. How could she find happiness when it had all been taken from her?

And it *was* her own fault, she reminded herself dejectedly. She had been infatuated by Angus and had allowed that infatuation to influence her life. Had it not been for Angus, she could have appealed to the Queen to allow her to stay at Larraig with her new husband. Had it not been for Angus, she would have welcomed marriage with Robin Drummond, and would not have wished to return to Court. Even if the Queen had commanded her, Margaret was romantic enough to have listened had she wished to stay with Robin. She was good and kind to her ladies, but she wanted Angus for herself. Too late Sarah was realizing how foolishly she had ruined her own life.

CHAPTER FOURTEEN

Although the threat of invasion had long since receded, Robin Drummond and his men rode to Larraig with great caution. Robin's keen eyes swept the landscape and he kept his party under cover wherever possible. The journey was made with all caution, but also without much delay so that Sarah was often weary to her soul as she sat in the saddle.

During their occasional stops, Sarah held herself aloof, having no maidservant to attend her, a fact which she considered the final indignity. Robin was treating her as though she, herself, were a maidservant. She longed to ask him about her father and grandmother, and about his own family, but he was in no mood to be questioned. He thought her still so ensnared by Angus that he would not listen. The King's life had been endangered and he could not hide his contempt.

When they finally came within hailing distance of Larraig, he made his usual careful routine check then rode beside her for a little way.

'I shall leave you at Larraig with your own people,' he told her. 'I am needed at Balwhidden. My father grows old and frail, and my brother has grown sick of his wounds. He is not sick to his death, but he will not be well enough to attend to Balwhidden until he is much stronger. It is a large estate and carries its full complement of rascals who would take advantage if they are not held in check. The farms could be neglected and the estate ruined if it is not properly managed.'

He was silent for a moment and she made no reply, having no wish to invite his contempt once again.

'My brother's wife is a gentle woman,' he continued, 'and even with my mother's help, she cannot hold Balwhidden for long. I have been there for some weeks, and have only left the place unguarded because I was summoned to attend my errant wife. Now I will leave Sir Thomas to deal with you as he sees fit. He is well and strong again and, I believe, quite capable of bringing discipline into your life, even if he recognizes that he attends to the matter later than he should. The child, Jamie, is of better behaviour though I have no doubt that his tutors take credit for that.'

Anger began to rise in her. Robin Drummond had said quite enough.

'You have humiliated me beyond endurance, sir,' she said in a choked voice. 'If you cannot be kind to me, then I pray you be silent.'

'*Kind* to you! Madam, my patience with you is extraordinary. If I were not tied hand and foot with Drummond affairs, I would soon know how to deal with you myself. Cannot you understand, even in the smallest degree, what it means to a Drummond to hear that his wife is cuckolding him with a rat like Angus?'

'That is *not* true!' she cried, passionately.

'Then they all lie? You were never alone in the courtyard with the man whilst the King sought his own pleasure, poor little one?'

She was silent.

'Well, Mistress?'

'That part is true, but...'

He turned away, snorting furiously.

'But not what you think!' she cried.

'You were forced? Are you trying to tell me that he forced his attentions upon you? By God, I will kill him!'

She was terrified. Robin was quite capable of challenging Angus, and what would happen then?

'You still do not understand! I was *not* forced. It was nothing...'

He turned to her and his looks were terrible.

'Nothing! I do not think you should say more, Mistress ... Mistress *Drummond*.' He ground out the name and she saw that his rage was now white hot. He was misunderstanding her completely and she shouted to him to try to make him understand.

'I tell you it was nothing! Nothing happen...'

His hands slapped across her mouth, knocking any further words, and suddenly a great calm fell upon her.

Very well, if he were determined to condemn her, then that is how it would be. She knew herself to be innocent and it was always more difficult to live with one's own guilt than to live with guilt imagined by other people. She had had so much love to offer Robin Drummond, but he did not want it. He did not want her. But she was tired of being wronged, of being mistrusted, of being falsely accused. She was Robin Drummond's wife and Sir Thomas Graham's daughter, but she was also herself, Sarah Drummond. She also had a duty to herself.

Sarah had wiped her face and tidied her hair and now she faced Robin proudly.

'I do not care for your opinion of me any more, Master Drummond,' she said. 'I know what I am and I know what is in me. I know what I have done and the mistakes I have made, but I have no reason for shame.'

'It pleases me that you think so highly of yourself,' he told her, heavily, and lifted his shoulders as he turned his head away. 'Now it seems that we arrive at Larraig.'

* * *

Sarah had been home at Larraig for almost a month when news came that the Queen Regent had married the Earl of Angus, and that the country's nobles were stunned into disbelief.

It had not been a happy time for her. Delighted though she was to see that her father had regained his strength, it had nevertheless given him the vigour to judge his daughter more harshly than he might. The wound in his head had healed, leaving him with an occasional severe headache and when that came upon him, Sarah knew that she must remain quiet and stay away from his immediate vicinity, or she would once again incur his displeasure.

'Why were you so foolish?' he would ask. 'You had cast your glances in the direction of Angus as anyone knew who was not a dunderhead, and that encouraged him to seek you out. Have you no more sense than to allow him to entrap you into such a situation as you have described to us, if you were completely innocent? And to do so when you were in charge of the King's person! By God, Mistress Drummond, it truly *is* treason. The Queen Regent is lenient with you, and with me since you are of my blood.'

His cheeks would flush and his eyes blaze with anger, so that Sarah grew afraid for him.

'You bear the good name of Drummond of Balwhidden who is now his brother's heir. Some day you will be Countess if he does not find a way of breaking the tie, which is what you deserve.'

'My brother-in-law, Archibald, is married and he has a young healthy wife. My husband is heir only until Archibald's wife bears sons.'

'He is sick of his wounds and cannot father children,' Sir Thomas told her, harshly. 'That is why Robin is required to administer to Balwhidden. Neil Drummond is old and frail and has lost an arm, his elder son is sick of his wounds, and Robin is in full charge of running the estate.'

'I see,' said Sarah. 'I ... I did not know.'

Pain pierced her heart. Robin would have even more incentive to try to be free of her if he became Earl of Balwhidden. The Earl was one of the country's more important nobles and it was not expedient for him to be out of favour with the Queen.

She was saddened, also, by the news that Archibald Drummond was now so sick, and had heartfelt sympathy for his young wife.

Lady Margaret had accepted her homecoming grumpily at first, then with secret relief. She was feeling her age again, and was glad to relinquish the reins of household management to Sarah. At first the maidservants had looked at her curiously and had been inclined to whisper in corners, but this Sarah would not tolerate. She informed John Dykes that any servant who showed lack of respect would be dismissed from service at once, and turned out of Larraig. For many Larraig was their only home and they were very comfortable within its stout walls with plenty of meat and warmth. Soon order was restored to the place, and Sarah afforded a new respect because of the firm stand she had taken.

'I thought to help you by sending a message to Lady Jane Hamilton,' her grandmother said, sadly. 'You were so much against a match with Drummond and I thought to remove you from here and back to Court where you had been happy.'

'Oh, Grandmother!' Sarah's eyes filled with tears. 'I knew my own heart when it was too late. I would have been so happy to be the wife of Drummond if only things had gone well for me, but he despises me now and he has angered me against him. I do not know why I admired the Earl of Angus. He is arrogant and he would have used me like a kitchen maid had I not fought him off.'

'You are not wily enough, child. At Court one must beware of enemies, and those who become jealous.'

'Mary Cunningham,' Sarah muttered. 'She was jealous of me. She might have married Robin had the match been arranged, but he was a younger son, and now he is heir to Balwhidden. Now he is a match for any lady at Court. He might annul our marriage, and take her for a wife.'

'Has he cause?' Lady Margaret asked, sharply.

Sarah blushed. 'No,' she said, simply.

'Then he will not do so. He is an honourable man and he would not lie, and he is also God-fearing. He will not seek an annulment.'

But he was also a very angry man, thought Sarah with a sudden chill to her heart, as she remembered the fury in his eyes when he accused her of encouraging Angus. An angry man might no longer be so honourable, or so rational.

*   *   *

As the weeks passed Sarah saw little of Robin who was concerned with affairs at Balwhidden, though occasionally he rode to Larraig and was closeted with Sir Thomas for many hours at a time. Sometimes other nobles joined them, and it was apparent to Sarah that there was unrest and dissatisfaction throughout the land because of the Queen's marriage to Angus.

The Douglases were now in charge of the young King and Lady Jane had been sent home to her family. Sarah thought about the old woman with love and affection, and knew how she must suffer now that she was deprived of looking after her 'wee mannie'. She had loved the child so very much.

Angus, as she learned, had grown swaggering and arrogant, and everyone knew that the Queen Regent no longer governed the country, and certainly not with the help of her previous ministers. Her every word had been, first of all, spoken by Angus. It was even rumoured around Court circles that her passionate love for him was coming to an end and that she had shown signs of hatred towards him. Some claimed that she bitterly regretted her hasty marriage.

Sarah's heart went out to the Queen as she listened to these rumours. She knew very well what the Queen was suffering now.

CHAPTER FIFTEEN

Sarah was kept busy as many guests rode into Larraig, most of them becoming more vociferous in their contempt for the present government.

'We need one of our own to govern our country,' Sir Thomas growled one day as Sarah organized a fine meal for a party of nobles in the Great Hall. Robin Drummond had also arrived that day, and sought her out briefly.

'We must have a talk,' he told her brusquely. 'I have been over-busy of late, but I am restoring my brother to some of his former strength. We have a physician who is better able to tend his wounds and is keeping the fevers at bay.'

'That is good news,' Sarah said, clearly. 'Then ... you may not always be the heir?'

She realized that she had spoken impulsively and perhaps not wisely when Robin turned to look at her with a hard, inscrutable look on his face.

'You sound as though that would please you,' he said, raising an eyebrow.

She said nothing. How could she explain that she wanted him as he was, and not as a powerful baron who was ashamed of his digraced wife. Seeing him again she knew that she still loved him and wanted him passionately despite his anger against her. She did not blame him for that. There had been too much evidence against her.

'It is not my business,' she said.

'Oh, but it *is* your business, Mistress Sarah. Can it be that you do not wish to bear future heirs for Balwhidden? Do you find that abhorrent to you?'

The colour rushed to her cheeks but she did not know how to answer him. If she confessed that bearing his children would be her dearest wish, he could easily turn on her with derision and her heart would be bruised and pained as it had been before.

She felt sick and unhappy at his nearness when she longed for him to take her in his arms and to feel the strength of his slender figure as he held her close. Why had she ever thought him a weakling? He looked paler than usual and worn with his responsibilities, but the strength of his personality shone through in the fine lines of his face and the bright blue of his eyes.

'By God, Madam, I shall be rid of Angus if it is the last thing I do,' he told her, harshly as she still remined silent. 'We owe no allegiance to him. But I will not touch you whilst your thoughts run to him.'

He turned away from her before she could tell him that she, too, hated Angus. He would not believe her however hard she might try to make him understand. He was in no mood to listen. Well, she would not beg for his favours, thought Sarah, as she raised her chin and went about her duties. She was more determined than ever to be true to herself.

She paused at the door, then turned to him where he stood kicking a log in the fireplace.

'You can think what you like!' she cried. 'If I am so little to you, it makes no difference.'

Then she turned and hurried along the stone passageway towards the kitchens.

* * *

'My thoughts turn to Albany in France,' said Sir Thomas as the nobles gathered together after the excellent meal for which Sarah received their praise gracefully.

'Albany?' Robin Drummond frowned a little. He was unsure that this was the correct man to have charge of their realm.

'Aye, John, Duke of Albany. His father was brother to our present King's grandfather, James Three, as you older men will remember. Now that was a strange business, if you like. James was jealous of both his brothers, Albany and Mar, and he soon had them under lock and key on any pretext, but Albany got away to France. He is dead now, God rest his soul, but his son, John, is there and has more right to be Regent of our country than any Douglas.'

The other nobles were silent for a while as they thought over this information.

'It is too soon to send for Albany,' Alexander Cameron objected. 'The King named Queen Margaret as Regent in his will and that was well witnessed. We must give her a proper chance, and she *is* sister to King Henry of England. We cannot risk upsetting him until we have gathered ourselves together after our rout at Flodden Field. None of us have forgotten that already, Thomas. We lost far too many men and we still lick our sores.'

Robin Drummond threw a log on the fire, then kicked it with his foot as Sarah had watched him do so often in the past. She knew that his mind was disturbed and he was trying to clear his thoughts.

'It is *not* the Queen Regent who is at fault,' he said. 'She is a good woman, doing her best if she listens carefully to the advice of her ministers before making judgements. But

Angus is trying for full powers, and he makes me sick to my stomach.'

'Aye, he has got himself puffed up with his own power,' Sir Thomas agreed.

One of the lesser noblemen moved uneasily as he looked at his companions.

'Albany is a Frenchman, whichever way you look at him,' he said, hesitantly, 'and I have heard that he owns a great deal of land in France through his mother. She was daughter to the Earl of Boulogne. Surely his main interest will be for France, and not for Scotland.'

'He is a hereditary duke of our kingdom,' said Sir Thomas, heavily. 'Why should he not owe allegiance to our Crown? It is his *duty* to act as Regent since in my opinion, the Queen has forfeited that right by her marriage to Angus.'

There were murmurs of assent all around the assembly of men.

'Lord Home supports the Queen,' Alexander Cameron put in. 'We would never get him to support our cause were we to put it to him. He would not add his name to any invitation to Albany, yet he would be a powerful supporter. He served well at Flodden Field and was victorious on the left wing.'

'Aye, but he served himself that day and did not offer help to the King, or any other division. I say we can disregard Home. Not everyone would support him,' said Sir Thomas.

'And I say that we should send a trusty messenger to France and find out if the Duke of Albany would be willing to take on such a responsibility as governing our country on behalf of the King, his cousin,' put in Alexander Cameron.

The other men moved again uncomfortably and regarded one another. It was one thing to talk amongst themselves and voice fears, one to another, but taking action was quite a different matter. Such a messenger, as they all knew, would have to be courageous and full of wisdom in order to present their case for such an invitation without inviting an accusation of treason.

'Such a man would need to have his wits about him,' Sir Thomas nodded.

'Then I propose Robin Drummond,' Alexander Cameron said, and Sarah, listening in the corner of the Great Hall, drew in her breath sharply. All eyes turned to Robin whose face went pale, though he did not flinch from their eyes.

'I could not leave Balwhidden until my brother's health has improved,' he said. 'Archibald is better, but not yet strong enough to get on his feet. He ... he has lost much vigour.'

'How long before he is well?' Hunter of Craiglaw asked.

'It is doubtful if he will ever be well, but I

would expect further improvement in three to four weeks,' Robin told them.

'It would be well for Robin to leave for France and be back before winter,' Sir Andrew Hunter advised. 'We can see by then if things improve in the government of our country. If they do not, then I think our most powerful nobles will be with us, and we can argue that the Queen forfeited the Regency when she married Angus.'

'She would be a thorn in the flesh of Albany were he to accept this charge laid upon him,' Alexander Cameron mused. 'His position would not be an easy one.'

'The Queen might choose to live at her brother's Court,' Sir Thomas suggested. 'I have heard that King Henry was not pleased with the marriage. He will not blame us for refusing to accept Douglas of Angus. He will respect us the more if we do not put up with him like a lot of humble peasants ... that is what Angus would make of us.'

Again there was silence then a few heads began to nod agreement.

'Will you accept the commission, Robin?' Sir Thomas asked, bluntly.

Robin stared round at every face and noted that they were all of one mind.

'That I will,' he agreed with a sigh, 'if it means putting that upstart back in his place. I do not owe allegiance to him, only to the King, and he has all my loyalty.'

'And that of your wife?' one of the lesser nobles asked in a jocular tone. This time the sudden silence was chilling as the winds which blew along the corridor.

'And that of my wife,' said Robin silkily.

'And my daughter!' Sir Thomas' tone was very robust.

Sarah had risen from a seat near the door where she had been stitching new household linen. Quietly she put it in her work-box, then bobbed a curtsey and made for the bedchambers. John Dykes could settle their guests for the night and no doubt there would soon be revelry if fresh wine was brought and tales of past glories began to be told. It was no place now for the ladies of the household.

She thought about Robin, and about his mission to France. She would see little of him in the future, though he had already told her he would not touch her because he believed she still pined for Angus. She would never convince him otherwise, she thought tiredly. Now she was so emotionally drained that she hardly cared any longer what he thought.

Her feelings seemed to have been wrapped up in blankets and were smothered so effectively that she no longer even felt pain or grief. She undressed and climbed into bed, then suddenly weak unhappy tears began to drench her cheeks as she tried to compose herself for sleep.

She remembered Lady Mary Cunningham

and how she had claimed to have seen the vision of the man in the azure-blue gown. Had the man appeared as a warning to the Queen Regent? Sarah wondered. Had the man been seeking the Queen to warn her not to marry Angus? Everyone had put the blame for his appearance on to herself and her neglect of the King's person. She would try to see Robin before he left for France, and try again to put this point of view to him. But would he listen? He would think she was merely trying to protect Angus again.

She drifted off to sleep, then suddenly she was awake again as a lithe, shadowy figure hung over the bed. Sarah began to scream, then a hand clamped over her mouth.

'Be quiet!' Robin hissed. 'Do you want to wake the dead? I leave for France as soon as I can arrange it, and I may not see you again before I leave. It will not be a trip for my own pleasure and there will be eyes and spies everywhere, though I am not too apprehensive regarding that. I have wriggled out of trouble before and will do so again.'

He had shed his clothing and had leapt into bed beside her.

'You are my wife, for better or worse, and it is time we did our duty by our families. My brother's wounds are such that he will leave no heir, but I will leave an heir for Balwhidden if it is the last thing I do! You will bear my child, Mistress Drummond, and do so willingly, or unwillingly, just as you choose.'

She had begun to fight him.

'I will not be used like one of your farm animals,' she cried, 'and have my child bred on me in hatred. If... if you despise me, then make a petition and be free of me and breed your children on a woman of your own choice. Someone like Lady Mary, for instance.'

'Lady Mary?'

'Cunningham. She told me you were in love with one another, only her family were against the match, but things have changed now that you are the heir to your estates.'

'So you would throw me to another woman.'

'If it made you happy. It was Lady Mary who saw the man in the blue gown, and blamed me for his presence at Court, saying it was a warning to protect the King, but suppose the warning was for the Queen, not to marry Angus.'

He was silent for a while, then his fingers dug into her shoulders.

'Always your thoughts turn to that man! Well, tonight you can forget him. Tonight you will honour your duties as my wife.'

Her heart leapt then hammered as he forced himself upon her. How often she had longed for his embrace, but she had not imagined him reaching for her in hatred and anger rather than love. The experience was painful so that she whimpered a little, but a few moments later he rose from her bed and donned his clothes.

'When you wake in the morning, I will be gone,' he said. 'I will leave you in peace.'

'Take care!' she cried, impulsively and he paused, then turned back to look at her.

'You do not want a fatherless babe? There will be plenty of people to care for you, and my own riches for the babe.'

She was silent. Despite his cruelty, she could not help feeling love for him, and that love appeared to have become confused with hatred. She no longer knew *how* she felt about him, she thought, as again her tears wet her pillow, but she only knew that he was the most important person in her life.

She hardly dared speak as the great lump in her throat slowly dissolved and the hot tears now flowed freely. Abruptly he turned and made for the door of her chamber, and now Sarah wept her heart out, then hurriedly left her bed and put on her robe. If he were travelling into danger in France, then she must tell him how much she cared for him, how much he meant to her. She must tell him the truth and try to make him understand that the Queen's new husband meant less than nothing to her.

But when she ran downstairs all was quiet except for one or two of the men guarding the house.

'Have you seen Master Drummond?' she asked one of them.

'He has ridden out for Balwhidden not a

minute ago,' she was told.

Sarah nodded then returned dejectedly to her chamber. Robin had gone. Why should she love him when he had said so clearly that he only wanted her to bear his child? He only wanted an heir.

Perhaps her body would disappoint him, she thought. There had been no child from their wedding night and fear clutched at her for a moment. She could well be a barren woman.

Well, that would serve him right, she thought defiantly, clutching at her pride once again. But ... the weeks would be long before he returned from France!

CHAPTER SIXTEEN

The weeks were long as the autumn weather gave way to a colder spell warning Sarah that winter was almost upon them. The trees blazed with colour all around Larraig, and provisions were being laid in against heavy snowfalls and poor conditions for travel.

As the weeks were passing, great unrest gathered amongst the nobles against the Queen's Regency, as Angus wrested more and more power into his own hands and many more waited for news from France to see if Albany would accept power, should the Queen be deposed.

At Larraig Sir Thomas moved around like a caged bear. He and Sarah had made a visit to Balwhidden to pay their respects to Sir Neil and Lady Elspeth Drummond. The Earl was now very old and frail and his memory much impaired as he and Sir Thomas talked together.

Archibald Drummond, Robin's older brother, was like a ghost of his former self. His skin was almost transparent and his hands as delicate as a girl's. His young wife, Madeleine, was a pale colourless girl who had always been shy and retiring. Now she spent all her days sitting with Archibald or with Lady Elspeth, and Sarah's heart was touched by their plight. She saw how much Robin was needed in this household when Madeleine came to sit with her.

'Archibald's days are long when Robin is not here,' she confided to Sarah. 'Robin will have to run Balwhidden when he comes home. Archibald can no longer take charge and Sir Neil is too old.'

'Cannot you interest Archibald in doing more to help himself?' Sarah asked. 'Does he not walk out now and again? Must he sit by the fireside all day?'

'He will not listen to me,' said Madeleine.

'Well, perhaps he will listen to me,' said Sarah. 'Robin will need a rest when he returns home and he should not be required to be nursemaid to Archibald. He is still the heir, you know, and I feel that he could be healthier if he chose to live a more healthy life.'

Madeleine's tired eyes opened wider.

'Would you speak to him, Sarah? He would only listen to Robin and he was better whilst Robin looked after him.'

'I do say so. If Archibald were my husband, I should put encouragement his way. I notice that he eats his meat with good appetite.'

'That is true.'

Madeleine leaned towards her and whispered:

'You know we will never have an heir?'

'I know.'

'I do not mind. I fear childbirth. My mother died when I was born.'

'Well, I do not intend to die having Robin's child,' said Sarah, roundly.

'Then ... then it is true that you are *enceinte*?' asked Madeleine and Sarah quickly put a finger to her lips as she looked round.

'I am not sure ... yet, though I think so.'

'I hope it is a boy for all our sakes,' said Madeleine. 'Archibald has suffered an agony of mind because he cannot hand on Balwhidden to his own children, but if he sees a new generation coming up for Robin, then I am sure he will be happy. That would improve his health more than anything else. It is important to the Drummonds.'

'I know,' said Sarah, bleakly. 'It has been made very clear to me.'

* * *

A week later she was sick in the mornings and old Anna Hyslop crowed with delight and rushed to inform Lady Margaret.

'So there is to be a child,' the old woman said with deep satisfaction. 'Balwhidden will be pleased, and your father, Sarah. Jamie grows so fast that he will soon be a man. It is a fine thing to have a child once again to gladden our hearts.'

'It appears to me that I must have a child to make everyone happy except myself,' said Sarah, bitterly, from the depths of her sick misery. No one had told her that a pregnancy could make her feel as though her last hour had come.

'What is this?' the old woman asked, peering at her short-sightedly. 'Are you yet such a bairn yourself that you cannot take pleasure in your own child?'

'Oh, Grandmother!' Sarah said, wearily. 'I do not know what gives me pleasure now.'

'Then drink Anna Hyslop's physic and go on your knees to the priest to say prayers for you. Sometimes I think you are an ungrateful young woman and that you do not appreciate your own good fortune. You are lucky that you do not rot in the dungeons at Edinburgh.'

Sarah's stomach heaved again and she turned a pallid face to Lady Margaret.

'I shall not live long enough to see any

dungeons,' she said. 'I am sick to my death.'

'Nonsense,' said Lady Margaret. 'We have guests riding in this day. Put cold water on your forehead, and attend to your duties. There is no time to pamper yourself.'

* * *

Gradually Sarah began to feel better and her life became less of a burden to her. As her health improved, she began to feel a great protective love for her coming child, and the happiness brought light to her eyes and a bloom in her cheeks. Her only sadness came in the long dark hours of the night when she sometimes woke crying for Robin, only to remember that he was no longer near and had no love for her as a wife. He only desired the child.

Sarah prayed for a daughter. A son would never belong to her. A son would be heir to Balwhidden from the day he was born, but a daughter would cling to her mother until a husband was found for her.

She called in the seamstress and ordered new gowns when her own no longer fitted her, and for once she showed interest in new styles and colours which would present her to best advantage. She followed Robin's example and washed off her sweats, combing out her long fair curls and drinking Anna Hyslop's herbal brews so that her black eyes sparkled with health.

Old Lady Graham watched her with silent satisfaction and even Sir Thomas softened towards her when he saw the new beauty of his only daughter.

*   *   *

Winter came upon them and it seemed to Sarah that Robin might remain in France until spring, and that Christmas may be celebrated at Larraig without him. With new authority as wife to the heir of Balwhidden, she managed the household servants with a very firm hand, and soon the kitchens were warm and fragrant with the preparation of meats for the Festive Season. The news was also better from Balwhidden in that Archibald had taken her advice and was walking out of doors in the clear crisp fresh air once again and that his health was better.

Sarah was directing the decorations of the Great Hall with sprays of holly, bright with berries, when word came that a party of horsemen were riding in. She prepared to welcome the travellers and to offer refreshment before they continued their journey since John Dykes had informed her that they were from Balwhidden.

'They will be serving Sir Neil or Lady Elspeth,' Sarah nodded. Many messengers passed their way on errands to and from Edinburgh.

Sarah tidied her hair, having removed her starched headdress, then put on a clean gown in creamy-coloured velvet with an over-dress of silk and lace to bring softness to her cheeks. It did not conceal her figure but Balwhidden already knew that she expected a child and had rejoiced happily in that knowledge.

As Sarah returned to the Great Hall, Robin was already there, his face pale and drawn with weariness, and the dust thick on his garments. He turned to look at her and she almost fainted with shock and reached for a chair to steady her trembling legs.

'Robin!' she whispered. 'I had not thought to see you before spring.'

'I was delayed,' he said, briefly. 'I was delayed in France. Where is Sir Thomas? I have news which must be discussed without delay.'

'He is collecting pheasants for Christmas fare. He will return shortly. I ... I will arrange food for you and your men.'

'And a wash,' he said. 'Have I fresh garments here at Larraig?'

'In our ... our bedchamber,' she said, nervously. 'I will call the maidservants and you can wash and change your clothing. I will help you.'

After satisfying his hunger, Robin shed his soiled garments and soon he was clad in fine linen and velvet. Sir Thomas had returned and had already sent out messages to his friends that Robin Drummond had returned from France with news.

It would take two days to gather together for a meeting, and when Sarah went to their bedchamber to supervise the removal of Robin's bath water and soiled garments, she found that he had thrown himself upon the bed and was fast asleep.

For a long time she stood looking down at him, noting the weary lines under his eyes and at the sides of his mouth. He looked older, but her love for him flowed afresh in her heart so that she could have taken him in her arms and kissed the warm sweetness of his lips. Then the treacherous jealousy came to eat at her heart. He had given no sign of pleasure at seeing her again. He had looked at her dully, then satisfied a ravenous appetite and divested himself of travel stains, but he had not attempted to touch her or to tell her he was pleased with the sight of her once again.

Why had he been delayed in France? She knew that the French ladies were very elegant and stylish and that they had few scruples in entertaining attractive visitors to the Court of France.

Sarah had already heard tales that it was mainly thanks to Queen Anne of France that King James had gone to war against England. She had flattered him and given him her garter. Perhaps Robin had spent many hours in the company of such ladies. Perhaps his wife looked dull and unattractive by comparison.

She leaned over him and suddenly his eyes flew open and she was staring into their blue depths. An arm as strong and hard as iron whipped round her waist and she was pulled down on to his chest.

'So,' he whispered, 'so I did very well by you. I see that we have made a child together.'

'Is that all you care about?' she asked, stormily. 'Am I nothing to you but a mother for your children? I suppose that I do not measure up to your fine French ladies and I am merely a rustic with none of the social graces. My hair lacks fashion and my clothes, and...'

'Be quiet!' he told her, grinning as he pulled her head on to his shoulder. 'You are fast turning into a shrew, my dear wife.'

He kissed her gently, then with passion as he began to pull her into bed beside him.

'We will disturb the babe,' she whispered.

'Not so. I am not such a dunderhead, and you are not such a sickly woman. In fact, I have never seen you in better health.'

'And you know too much already about such matters, Robin Drummond.'

'It is well for you that I do. I know that jealousy means that you are not so indifferent to me as you have led me to believe, and I have never seen a finer display of a jealous woman than you have just given to me. It occurs to me that perhaps you might even be passionately in love with me.'

'Why should I love you when you do not even care for me? You only want...'

'I know. A mother for my children. I already have a mother for my child, and now I want a wife to share my love. Certainly I have loved other women, but that is all in the past and best forgotten. Now I only love my wife.'

'How can I believe you?' she whispered.

'I was jealous also. Was I not eaten up with jealousy over Angus? I wanted to kill him. I wanted to throw him against a wall and break his neck, as I am skilled enough to do. Instead I have taken part in a plot to wrest power from his hands and ruin his government of our country. Perhaps that is a more noble punishment.'

'But I never loved him after I married you, Robin,' she told him, earnestly. 'I only loved you, and I was jealous of Lady Mary Cunningham.'

'She is a sad lady, that one. She is not a strong-minded woman and has fancies where none exists. She was wrong if she told you I loved her, because I did not, though I knew that she would have welcomed love.'

'Then you do not think she saw the man in the azure-blue gown? Do you think she only imagined that?'

'I do not know. Perhaps she did. I do know that I will spend my life protecting our rightful King. Albany is willing to rule Scotland as

Regent, and I shall say so to your father and the other nobles, but I am glad he is not heir to our throne,'

'Why so?'

'I cannot say why I should say so, but I think he could be easily influenced by others. He is a weak man in my opinion, but he is passionate for our cause in removing Queen Margaret and Angus. It is not for me to have the final word as to whether he be invited to come to Scotland, or not, but that is why I delayed my visit in France before returning to Scotland. I needed more time to assess Albany and to make up my mind as to his true nature.'

'And?'

'I shall advise caution.'

'They will not take your advice. They are all avid for change. The Queen Regent and Angus grow more unpopular by the hour.'

'We waste time,' said Robin suddenly. 'Are you truly my wife and will accept me in love? Because I have always loved you, Sarah Graham, who is now Drummond. I thought you despised me for a weakling.'

'I learned better,' she said, blushing. 'I learned to love you, Robin Drummond, and I am glad to receive you in love. I wanted a daughter who would remain close to her mother, but now I wish your child to be a son, for you.'

'We will have many children, sons and daughters. We will hold Larraig for your brother, then you will be required to live at Balwhidden, my dear wife. Will that be unwelcome to you?'

'I shall be happy wherever you are, Robin.'

They lay happy and contented in one another's arms. Sarah now knew the true strength and passion of her husband as well as his gentleness and love. Now she had no doubt about that love for her which was as great as her own for him, and she felt humble that she belonged to such a man.

Soon there may be changes in the government of their country and Robin was not wholeheartedly in favour of these changes, but always he would serve the King, just as she, herself, wished to serve the King whom she still loved as she would one day love her own son.

Robin had fallen asleep again, worn out by adventures which would be told and retold round the huge log fire in the Great Hall as all their friends gathered to listen.

Sarah slipped to her knees beside the bed and gave thanks for his safe journey home, and for the gift of his love.